WILLOWIST

THE RETURN OF THE THIRD REICH

A thrilling novel about senior citizen Nazi hunters.

Correale Frank Stevens

CORREALE FRANK STEVENS *has served as an elected member of the PA House of Representatives, District Attorney, trial judge and is currently a judge on the appellate PA Superior Court of PA. He is an author, college adjunct, lecturer and television personality, appearing on the Judge Stevens Show and on Veterans' View.*

www.correalestevens.com

This book is dedicated to
Maxton, Rocco, Noah, Ella, Elsie and Madelyn.

WP
Willowist Publishing LLC

*The Dark cannot claim
what the Light does not surrender.*

C.L. Wilson

*By the tree the fruit is known.
An evil tree cannot bring forth good fruit.*

Abraham Lincoln

PROLOGUE

HAMBURG, GERMANY

October. 1941. The principal saw them first. The black Mercedes SUV, stopped in the "No Parking" area reserved for school buses. The SS uniforms and long, black leather coats with Nazi symbols. The men, one whose uniform with decorated insignias looked to be the leader, walked crisply toward the elementary school main door.

The principal closed his office door, turned off the lights and sat rigidly in his desk chair. Shakily, he opened his desk drawer, pulled out a flask filled with whisky and took a long swig. His hands trembled, and he started to feel the sweat on his face. He knew the stories. The concentration camps, the gas chambers, the torture. They had been at the school before. They marched past his door, looking straight ahead. He collapsed in his chair. Who would be their victim this time, he thought.

The school teacher heard the footsteps, the unmistakable "click click" of the boots on the hardwood floor. As the footsteps grew louder and louder, he told the students he would be leaving them for awhile and that he loved them all.

The teacher quickly ran down the hall into a storage room. Just as in practice drills he climbed into an empty waste container, pulled the lid closed and sat quietly.

The Nazis began a systematic search of every classroom looking for the teacher. Some of the sixth graders began to cry, several stood up and gave the Heil Hitler salute.

He felt the whoosh of the air as the door burst open to the storage room. They began emptying the storage bins and found him crouched down inside the bin. The Nazis pointed their guns at him. There were four of them. Before he passed out, he felt a slight sting as the rag was placed over his mouth. Without a word, they carried him down the school hallway toward the SUV past classrooms with teachers cowering at their desks.

The teacher awoke, with such intense pain in his hands and feet he passed out again, briefly.

As his eyes focused he saw a line of fifteen or twenty women and children gunned down by Nazi soldiers.

He vomited as he saw gasoline poured on a man who was then set on fire.

Through his drug-induced state, it took him a moment to realize something was very wrong. He was upright, but not standing. He could move his head, but not his hands and feet. He had difficulty breathing, his chest heaving back and forth. Why were those people beneath him looking up at him?

As he looked down he saw the shocking reality. He had been crucified!He had been staked alive on a cross, nails hammered into his hands and feet and the cross lifted erect at the concentration camp site.The pain was horrifying, every part of his body felt on fire.He mumbled a prayer, and his body went limp. The Nazis had eliminated another member of the Resistance movement in Germany.

CHAPTER 1

WILLOWIST RETIREMENT CAMPUS, USA

Sophia opened the door to the bedroom and nodded approvingly when she saw the king size bed, off-white antique dresser and mirror, walk-in closet. A fully furnished condo with a guest bedroom, spacious living room and sliding glass door leading to a deck. She had chosen the third floor, the highest. Everything is just as promised in the Willowist brochure. An Active Adult community.

She laughed. They had no idea just how "active" she was for a 60's something senior citizen. Sophia Jansenn. Her bio for Willowist lists her as a "Retired State Department vice-president of customer operations." She laughed again. Even the most sophisticated internet and background search into her background would disclose only that but she led a quiet, boring, bureaucrat life. Nothing reported about assassinations. Afghanistan. Iraq. Undercover assignments.

***

Sophia reminisced back to the 1950's when she was growing up in a village in Iowa, which bordered on the

Mississippi River. She missed that fresh grown corn and riding the tractor with her dad on the family ranch.

"Sophia, get those dirty boots off right now," Lilly Jansenn exclaimed. "Really, hasn't Pop taught you to not track dirt all over my kitchen floor?"

Lilly took care of her husband, Donnie Jansenn, their daughter Sophia, son Donnie Jr and just about anything that needed attention in the household. As serious a person as Lilly was, Donnie had an easy going calm manner which belied his hard physical work on the ranch.

Donnie was hard of hearing from his infantry duties in WWII, and the everyday shouting around the house was normal and not argumentative. A young Sophia thought her parents were fighting and had been frightened the first few times she heard her parents talking loudly until Lilly explained the situation.

Lilly and Donnie passed on their intense patriotism and traditional values to Sophie and Donnie, Jr. Both children were determined to join the military and serve their country.

"Ok, Mom. Sorry. Can I go into town tonight with Viola? It's Friday and her dad will give us a ride there and home."

"10 pm, Sophia. Home. And none of that Elvis Presley music, he's a flash in the pan, won't last long in the music business. He wouldn't know a hound dog if he tripped over one."

"I saw you watching him on Ed Sullivan, you were watching him shake his legs," Sophia laughed. "You hush now child!," Lilly said as she blushed bright red.

At the diner Sophia and best friend Viola Lepere ordered their usual milkshakes and fries. Sophia put some nickels in the juke box player, and Elvis Presley's "Don't Be Cruel" came on.

The Hash Brown Diner was the only gathering spot for young people in the village. The back room area had booths surrounded by a slightly sunken, one step down wooden dance floor. The biggest controversy in years in the town was the 50 cent cover charge the owners charged to sit in the booths on weekend nights, especially after football games when the teenagers came in droves.

Sophia and Viola spent many days together as Lilly and Viola's mom lived on neighboring farms and were close friends. Sophia remembered the time they were kids and took two S&G green stamps books to the store thinking they could get new bicycles. And the time in third grade they were sent to the principal's office for laughing in class and couldn't stop giggling in front of Mrs. Harris, the principal.

One particular summer night Sophia and Viola were riding bareback. "Come on, Sophia. You fraidy cat!" Viola yelled as she crossed a creek that had become swollen with recent rains. Sophia reined up before the creek and watched in shock as Viola and her horse were swept downstream in the water. "Sophia. Help!", Viola cried. Sophia dived into the water ahead of Viola and Hammer, her horse, and was able to unhook Viola's feet from the stirrups. Viola was limp.

She dragged Viola ashore and gave her mouth-to-mouth until Viola sputtered out the water. Hammer was able to work free of the creek but was traumatized and had to be put down with a broken leg. Viola recovered and swore she would never be reckless again, and it was thanks to Sophia's pleading with Viola's mom that Viola wasn't grounded. "Friends forever!", Viola had said to Sophia.

Sophia shook her head at the double locks on her Willowist apartment door, remembering how doors were never locked in her home growing up.

"So many changes in life," she thought. Drinking water from a hose. Milk poured out of real glass bottles. Blackjack and Teaberry gum. School classes beginning with the Lord's Prayer and the Pledge of Allegiance. Monkey bars at the school playground. Respect for elders. All gone.

As she looked around her new high tech, all amenities Willowist apartment she wondered if anyone else there once had a "party line" telephone service with a real live telephone operator.

"Jansenn, in for Morgan." Sophie slapped Charlie Morgan's hand as she took his place on the basketball court. She was the first girl allowed on the intra-mural basketball team, and the boys teased her until she out-dribbled and out-shot most of them.

Viola was more interested in dance recitals while Sophia excelled in sports. Taller than the other girls, faster than many of the boys, academically gifted, Sophia was getting attention from college admission staff, basketball scouts and military recruiters. And especially from Scotty Townsend, the high school idol of every girl at the school.

"Come on Jansenn," Scotty whispered in math class. " Just a movie, as friends."

"Knock it off, Scotty. You had your chance but cheated on me. With that loose Amanda Fredden. Remember, she mocked me in front of my friends saying I didn't know how to keep a guy? Besides, Viola is my best friend, your girlfriend, and I have told you a hundred times, no way Jose will I cheat with you on her!"

Scotty laughed but Sophia was the one girl he wanted and couldn't get.

Not long after, Sophia met with the United States Marines recruiter and couldn't wait to join. Donnie, Jr. was killed as an "advisor" in Vietnam before the large scale American troops were sent. Donnie was in the first wave of Americans supposedly there to train South Vietnamese troops and not engage in combat. He was lying in his bunk when two Viet Cong stormed into the tent and took him in front of the villagers. They set him on fire and warned the villagers that's what happens to any Americans and South Vietnamese who support them.

Sophia hated the protestors for not supporting the troops, and she organized a pro-military rally at her high school. Students sang the National Anthem and marched through the halls. Even Principal Harris joined in.

Sophia received her college training courtesy of the Marines and became an officer. Exceptionally talented with weapons, she was accepted into a Special Ops secretive unit which was one of the units that infiltrated enemy strongholds.Several of the units are now, thanks to Sophia's persistent lobbying of her commander, composed of senior citizen veterans who remain patriotic, had exemplary prior service, security clearances and maintained an appropriate physically fitness level.

In her last assignment in Kabul, Sophia and her team member Betty Ann Bodner went undercover as elderly Muslim women and infiltrated a group of Taliban leaders. Despite the increasing urbanization of Kabul, vestiges of the Taliban had remained. This particular group preyed on young girls and engaged in human trafficking to obtain weapons in return.

The assignment had begun with a wild cab ride careening throughout the streets. Sophia kept getting slammed from one side of the cab to another while the driver weaved in and out of traffic. Seat belts were not the custom in Kabul, she remembered thinking.

As Sophia and Betty Ann approached the row of shacks on the targets' street, they walked slowly with Burka on and heads down. Respectful Muslim women. But each one with a nine round Colt Commander pistol under her garment.

The door to the shack opened before she knocked, and there were two Arab men waiting for her to give them a list of girls to be kidnapped for the trafficking operation. She bowed slightly but neither one returned the courtesy.

"Are you two alone", the overweight one asked.

"Yes."

"The list?", as he allowed her into the room where there were two other Arab men sitting at a table smoking and drinking.Several assault rifles were on the table, and Sophia was well aware these men would probably murder Betty and her once the men got what they wanted.

In a respectful tone Sophia replied,"Here is the list. Do you have money for me?"

The overweight one handed the list to one of the men at the table, a man she noticed had shaky hands.

While Shaky Hands looked at the list of the girls and studied a map, Sophia raised her Colt pistol and put a hole in the head of Shaky Hands.The overweight one was able to get a shot off and hit BettyAnn but Sophia quickly killed him and the remaining men. The silencer on Sophia's weapon worked perfectly but she hesitated a moment to see if anyone else was in the building. All quiet. Sophia had just eliminated the leaders of a major trafficking group.

The Taliban men terrorized local families and paid money to young men who kidnapped girls for the trafficking ring. Most of the girls were sent to Russia where they were bought by wealthy men and kept in captivity for sex. Girls as young as 12 were targeted.

Sophia gathered their laptops and files with information that would lead to freedom for hundreds of young girls being held by the Taliban. Betty Ann died in Sophia's arms. Sophia knew the risks of their work but quietly sobbed.

Betty Ann was not the only teammate to die. Sophia knew when she and James became involved it was not a good idea. One of the first rules of the military is to not get romantically involved with teammates. They did their best not to fall in love but love happened in her younger days.

They were stationed in a town on the Amalfi coast to do surveillance on the town's mayor. They enjoyed Italian markets and cafes, hotel rooms overlooking the ocean. James could fight hand-to-hand combat but caress her tenderly. Many evenings sitting on the hotel porch they talked about life after the military. Settling down in the Midwest, maybe invest in a small ranch. Have some kids. Raise a family. Sophia was happy.

Six months later James and Sophia were assigned to Iraq. Their encampment was invaded by hostile Iraqi. James had been on patrol, and when James and his team returned, a firefight started. Sophia was grabbed by one of the hostiles, and James hit him with the butt of his rifle but the hostile plunged a knife into James' stomach. James whispered "I love you" to Sophia as he lay dying. From that day forward Sophia swore off relationships. She would never meet another man she could love as much as she did James.

Sophia's thoughts returned to Willowist. She wondered what the prim and proper ladies she was to join at dinner tonight would think if they saw her assassinating Taliban leaders or lobbing a hand grenade into a Taliban-controlled shack.

Her living conditions in Afghanistan consisted of a one room cement block with bed, sink and toilet. No daily maid service, no buffets and Happy Hours, no amenities like at this undercover assignment.

***

Sophia was bemused to see the pampering of the residents at Willowist, several five star restaurants, the movie theater with reclining seats and full food and drink service, the fitness center and daily gentle exercise classes. The bus trips to the city. The men downing the viagra pills for Friday nights socials with the ladies. The chandeliers in the dining room, hallways and bookshelves lined alcoves.Some retirement community!

For her first dinner at Willowist, she chose a white blouse and khaki skirt. Sophia tied her shoulder length dark brown hair above her head and nodded approvingly as she took one last look in the full length mirror. No need to hide her natural beauty this assignment. If anything, she could still turn a man's head. But she had no problem being covered with mud, crawling through a field with her assault rifle and backpack when her assignment required her to do so.

At 5'8" Sophia preferred flats so as not to be towering over men, especially the other senior citizens here, some of whom were lively and active in spite of various physical disabilities. She wanted to look like a classy, low-key senior citizen while downplaying her physically fit, slender, muscular body.

As competent with an AR15 automatic weapon as well as with a kitchen recipe, Sophia had portrayed many different looks and roles in her previous assignments over her career. Bank teller, accountant, lawyer, secretary, assassin. But for this assignment she is simply a retired, 60 something financially-independent senior citizen. It was Sophia's persistent lobbying efforts with her commander and a powerful and friendly congresswoman that several secretive task forces in the military were created, consisting of physically fit, former military, senior citizens. Tonight she would meet her teammates, all undercover at Willowist.

By force of habit,she carefully placed her favorite Glock into the shoulder holster, covered by her Navy blue blazer. The senior citizens here are not exactly ISIS, she smiled, as she looked again in the mirror.

She knew she would have to deal with Viola Lepere's presence at some point.But former best friend or not, she would not allow Viola to do anything to jeopardize the mission.

One final look in the mirror.She was ready for her first Early Bird dinner at Willowist. And having grown up as a fan of James Bond movies, she placed a small marker by her door, if it was moved upon her return, someone had entered her apartment.

Time to get to work.

CHAPTER 2

TEL AVIV

The nondescript building in the Israeli suburb with the hidden parking area in the rear and the faded "JJ Petroleum" sign outside was anything but abandoned. Several interior offices with state-of-the art tracking gear, computers and satellite phones were manned by Bri staff. The 5-14-48 Brigade headquarters. Or the Bri as it was known to the members. The name pays homage to when Israel was recognized as a nation, May 14, 1948. And their mission is to track down and eliminate any living Nazis. Not trusting captured Nazis to the legal system, the Bri quietly executed them, 3 shots to the head. The calling card of the Bri.

Ross Fetterman, a veteran of Israeli Army Intelligence founded the group, and allied with several well-heeled financiers, established the military unit independent of the Israeli government. Fetterman committed his team to following every lead, no matter how credible, no matter where in the world to finding and eliminating former Nazis.

JoJo Gantz was second in command, a feisty 5'3 dynamo, fearless in combat. Responding to attacks on

Israeli communities by Palestinian guerrillas based in Syria, Lebanon and Jordan, Israel dealt a decisive blow to the threats of those groups to invade Israel and established itself as the region's preeminent military power.

JoJo's parents were soldiers in the Six Day War in 1967, and both were recognized for their exemplary service. The Six Day War was the result of continued tension between Israel and its Arab neighbors. Egypt closed the Straits of Tiran and mobilized forces along the border with Israel. Israel caught the Egyptians by surprise and destroyed their airfield as well as securing ground forces supremacy.

The guerrillas were no match for the Israeli military as Egypt suffered 11,000 casualties, Jordan 6000 and Syria 1000, while Israel's losses were limited to 700.

Not long ago Gantz had led the team to a farmhouse in the Alsace region of France. She had learned of a gathering of twenty-two high level leaders in the neo-Nazi movement.

"Take the shots after I get to the back of the building and throw the smoke bombs in from the rear door" she ordered her teammates. "There are only two guards. Be ready to shoot anyone who comes out of that door, no exceptions. If they are in there, they are Nazis."

As JoJo was crawling through the field to the side of the building a startled barn cat meowed and jumped out of the high grass. JoJo froze as one of the guards came around the corner to investigate. "It's just a stupid cat," the guard laughed and put a bullet in the cat. The guard returned to the front of the buildings, and JoJo found a vantage point for her sniper attack.

Inside the farmhouse the Nazis had set up folding chairs and a podium in the farmhouse living room. The discussion centered around upcoming plans for the Nazi groups. Each Nazi group, referred to as a cell, had ten members and did not know the names or specific locations of other cells. The system was set up to frustrate any attempt by Interpol to use the arrest of one cell members as a bargaining chip to find others. All the cells had access to a secure website, including a chat room.

"We are in a constant communications with the High Command in Germany, the speaker began. "Our leader, Franz Worthermann will give us the approval to move forward at his chosen time. Each of you are assigned a ranking government official in France to assassinate on the signal of Commander Worthermann. By coordinating the executions to occur in different parts of France at the same time, this will create fear and confusion here and draw attention away from the planned event in the States. Comrades, we are." His voice trailed off as the smoke bombs exploded, and he screamed "Fire! Fire! Get out!"

On her signal the snipers shot each guard, and just as expected the Nazis ran out the door, to be shot dead by JoJo and the other snipers. Three shots to the forehead of each Nazi, the telltale sign of the Bri.Another successful mission for JoJo Gantz.

JoJo Gantz was always a fighter. During her time at a college in the States she was subjected to anti-Semite remarks by other students. She was charged on several occasions with assault but the charges were all dismissed on the legal theory of self defense. Gantz never initiated a fight but did not hesitate to engage the aggressor, who usually ended up in the local hospital ER.

Not the best student, Gantz was the star shooter on the college rifle team. She had an innate ability with guns and could field strip a weapon faster than her instructors. As classmates learned more about her abilities with weapons, the anti-Semite slurs stopped.

In her senior year, she was named College Student of the Year for her heroic efforts in saving dorm students from a fire. Gantz awoke to the smell of smoke and alerted the entire dorm to evacuate. Several female students were trapped in the stairwell, and Gantz smashed her way into the stairwell area and rescued the students, carrying them out one by one. Gantz suffered from smoke inhalation but was treated by the arriving firefighters, who lauded her for her bravery.

Her reputation grew as she became a fearless and feared member of the Israeli military. Fetterman recruited her for the Bri. Her familiarity with military procedures and strategy, as well as her ability with weapons, led to her leading missions. Gantz relished seeking out and eliminating old WWII Nazis or more recently the neo-Nazis who were becoming more active.

"What do you know about a retirement community in the States, called Willowist," Fetterman asked her.

"Not a thing. Why? Whats up?"

"Don't know. It's being mentioned in some secure chat rooms we hacked into where Nazi sympathizers hang out. Maybe a couple of old Nazis hiding out there."

"Willowist. I'll do some research on it, maybe pay a visit there."

CHAPTER 3

WILLOWIST

Sophia had studied the daily ebb and flow of the operations at Willowist and knew exactly where George Mattes would be seated. His usual table in a corner, where he was occasionally joined by a few ladies, but mostly he enjoyed eating alone. Tonight he was reading a book about about a tech nerd who often hacked into conversations among members of organized crime. George wanted to be the one who discovered who killed Jimmy Hoffa and the location of the body. He was embedded for this assignment three months ago as a Special Ops team member, did not yet meet his fellow undercover agents.

George's family owned a couple of dress factories, and as soon as he was old enough, he worked with basic accounting tasks. Accounts receivable. Sending out invoices. Making the deposits. But he was destined for more. His SAT scores in math were in the top 1% and earned him a fully paid scholarship to MIT.

Not a fan of the Vietnam War but patriotic, he didn't complain when he was drafted right after college. George's abilities kept him out of the jungle warfare and instead led him to intelligence work. As he entered middle age, unlike many of his contemporaries, he embraced technology and the growth of the computer and internet devices. He continued to work for the federal government and was chosen to serve in Homeland Security before his senior citizen status moved him into the special-ops senior division and his current assignment at Willowist.

George was a highly trained operative, although not involved in the more violent end of missions. An incredibly gifted techie, George had hacked into the most secure banking and governmental websites in the world. Fluent in several languages, George had an important role in monitoring internet chat among terrorist groups. Facial recognition software, use of drones to follow live events, George could do it all.

One time he was trying a new drone over a street in Buffalo, NY at the same time bank robbers were entering their get-a-way car. He watched the car's escape route live on his computer with the drone overhead following it and called the state police, giving them live updates on the car location. After the police intercepted the robbers, he shut down the drone, and the state police knew someone helped them but George and his computer address remained anonymous.

The recent rise of neo-Nazism had gotten the attention of his superiors. George was assigned to hack into suspected pro-Nazi chat rooms and report on their activity. In the last six months or so, the Nazi internet activity was higher than it had ever been, and Willowist was somehow important to their movement. George was assigned undercover to learn how important.

George preferred assignments where he didn't have to socialize. Put him in a war room with monitors and computers, and he was at his best. Willowist, however, unnerved him at times. With a shortage of male residents, the women flirted shamelessly with every man available. Just last week Alma Woodruff, in her blonde wig and bright red lipstick almost got into a fistfight with Esther Chaney over sitting at George's table for breakfast. George ate breakfast faster than he ever had in his life!

George was awkward around women and was not used to competition for his attention. Except for when his nerves act up and cause his right eye to twitch slightly, George was a somewhat physically handsome nerdy looking guy, intelligent and healthy for his 60's some years.

Alma declared George "her man" and frequently tried to engage George in conversation, hand rubbing his shoulder or touching his arm when she spoke. Every night for the first two weeks she knocked on his door, "Are you all right, George? Do you need a tuck in? If you let me in I will cuddle with you until you go to sleep." Without opening the door George answered "Goodnight, Alma. I am fine." His eye twitched rapidly.

She finally turned her attention to Mickey Sustek, an 84 year old, wealthy former tow truck company owner who enjoyed Alma's attention. Mickey owned a company that towed tractor trailers that had become disabled for one reason or another. Like many other men at Willowist, Mickey was a widower, and Alma's flirtations worked on him.

George, though, was always first on Alma's list, and every day she had some cute remark for him, which consistently unnerved him. Other women were afraid of

Alma. According to whispered discussions in the Gossip Room, Alma had potential for violence and had been institutionalized.

Never confirmed by anyone at Willowist but a rumor repeated enough to be thought true, Alma was married to a mailman and lived a modest lifestyle. She had a violent temper and often physically beat up her husband. He took her to court and was granted a Protection From Abuse court order. Alma was to move out of the house and could have no contact with her husband. A week later her husband was severely beaten and permanently disabled. While there was not enough evidence to arrest her, Alma was committed to a mental hospital for a sixty day period, then released.

She was in line at a grocery store lotto machine, and the lady in front of her "forgot something at the deli" and left the line. Alma's ticket won $5 million dollars and after taking a few cruises, she joined the Willowist community. The lady who would have won the lottery demanded some of the money but Alma punched her in the face and walked away smiling.

When Alma was present, women were careful to stay away from George.

Alma grew up in a rural area with a family that struggled financially. She had none of the childhood toys other kids in her class had and was always dressed in old clothes. Her mother was an alcoholic and her father abandoned her mom and her when Alma was three years old. She had few friends in school and constantly dealt with anger issues. She was expelled from a junior high school for provoking fist fights with other girls. Her conduct escalated to the time she trashed a classroom and attacked a teacher for no known reason. Alma was in and out of mental institutions.

"She is nouveau riche trailer trash," Esther said to the ladies at her table. "She was in line to buy a lottery ticket, and the lady in front of her got tired of waiting to buy a ticket and left for the deli. Wouldn't you know it! Alma's ticket ended up being worth $5 million dollars. If the lady hadn't left the line, Alma would be back in her trailer instead of here. I can't stand her." The other ladies preferred not to antagonize Esther who was known for sarcastic comments even to her friends, and instead they turned their attention back to watching George's table.

"May I join you?" Sophia extended her hand. George's eye twitched.

"Of course," he said as he looked up from his book, startled at Sophia's beauty.

"George Mattes", as he stood and offered a chair to Sophia. Some of the other female residents eagerly watching George's table noticed he was momentarily flustered by Sophia's sophisticated beauty but he recovered quickly.George had been briefed and knew Sophia was to be his team leader for his assignment.She was much better looking in person than on the pictures in the portfolio his superiors had given him in advance of the assignment.

Keeping secure protocol and knowing other residents were watching, he asked "I haven't seen you before, are you new to Willowist?" What wasn't protocol was the slightly high-pitched voice he heard coming out of his mouth."Damn, where did that come from", he thought.

"Yes. I am Sophia Jansenn, and this is my first dinner here, I hope I am not disturbing you."

"Not at all," George replied, in a deeper, controlled voice. "I prefer company to reading", he lied.

More quietly to Sophia: "I have some news to share later."

Sophia ordered a glass of pinot grigio. "Once we meet our third team member we'll plan our course of action."

George took a sip of brandy and relaxed, the twitching stopped. "I'll show you my computer setup, very secure.It looks like a plain laptop but once the code is entered, it uses a secure built in wifi and will give us access to all our servers and other substantial resources. I have a couple of drones in my private locker in the basement for use when needed.Everyone at Willowist gets a private locker for storage, I reset the combination lock so no one can access but me. I don't trust the Administrator here. The drone does live streaming to my secure website. I can follow a car, spy on a house, whatever we need."

Just as Sophia anticipated from her research into Willowist, Lady Victoria Constantine, her short black hair sprinkled with gray approached the table and sat down. Wearing a subdued red sweater with a black skirt, and pearl necklace she extended her hand.

"Hi, you must be Sophia."

Lady Vikki considered herself as a one woman welcoming committee and knew everything about everybody at Willowist.She didn't hesitate to violate the privacy of others and rumored to be having an affair with the Willowist administrator, she had access to the codes of every apartment door and occasionally entered apartments without the resident's consent. Sophia knew to be wary of her.

Not really an English lady, Lady Vikki was the daughter of German immigrants and the widow of a wealthy Greek entrepreneur. One of the reporters for the society columns had dubbed her "Lady Vikki", and the nickname stuck.

Lady Vikki grew up in Los Angeles as a trust fund baby. Her father had made money in the mining industry in Germany and immigrated to the United States after WWII. Lady Vikki's father had business ties to some of the Nazi leaders, who helped his financial success.

A regular donor to right wing extremist groups internationally, Lady Vikki was on a Homeland Security watchlist. Sophia's research disclosed Lady Vikki could be cold, calculating and dangerous. Tonight, though, she was just charming and social.

George, Lady Vikki and Sophia chatted throughout dinner not entirely oblivious to the murmuring of a group of female residents who were watching their table with interest. "Georgie boy is getting some tonight,"Esther Chaney whispered to her table group. "That new woman is pretty."

"Many have tried but no one has succeeded," chimed in Suzy Petuch. "She better watch out for Alma!"

"George is quite the lady's man," Lady Vikki nodding toward the table of ladies watching them intently, laughingly disclosed to Sophia. "They all want his company but he is a loner."

George blushed, eye twitched. "I came to Willowist to relax, Lady Vikki, not to be a socialite."

"My apology. Everyone here respects you and your privacy." "Except me. I don't respect anyone's privacy," she thought but didn't say.

Sophia's first Willowist dinner in the formal Leonardo da Vinci Room was beyond what she anticipated. Fine dining with Venetian style furniture, such as dining tables made of imported maplewood and palms of olive wood with inlaid tiles complemented by plush French dining chairs. The walls were lined with reproductions of paintings by da Vinci, Raphael, and Michelangelo all completed the Renaissance theme.

First choice on the menu with gold-plated large print letters was consommé or French onion soup, followed by mixed green salad and dinner entre choice of salmon, breaded stuffed pork chops or a vegetarian selection.

Wine was offered at every lunch and dinner, although some of the residents selected highballs and other mixed drinks. The desert menu included homemade pies, chocolate eclairs, and rainbow ice cream.

Residents could enjoy a lighter fare in the more casual Hot Shoppe named after a 1950's food chain. The ladies still dressed to the max here, flirting with every man who ventured into the cafeteria style dining room. As a throw back to the 1950's, the booths had individual tabletop juke boxes with music from various artists and groups like Perry Como, Gene Pitney, Roy Orbison, Little Anthony, the Ponytails and, Sophia's favorite of course, Fabian.

Sophia finished her after-dinner Amaretto and invited George and Lady Vikki to show her around the gardens.Sophia wanted to learn as much about Lady Vikki as she could as well as observe the Willowist layout firsthand. Sophia had detailed maps of Willowist but wanted to see the facility firsthand.

"I am a little tired but I will see you at breakfast. George, will you be so kind as to show this beautiful lady the grounds?" Lady Vikki said her goodnights.George blushed, eye twitched, as he walked away with Sophia.Some of the ladies in the dining room were surprised George was more attentive to Sophia than he was to anyone else at Willowist. To the ladies, Sophia looked to be successful in making a move on George.

Approaching the front of the main building one drives around an 4 acre man-made lake outfitted with over 800 nozzles and 2,500 lights.The lights change colors randomly and there are benches on the walkway around the fountain for residents to relax and enjoy the colors and sounds of the cascading waters.

The rear of the main building,also contained carefully manicured and landscaped grounds.French doors on the rear of the bulding's large wraparound porch led to pathways through colorful gardens and a circle of small fountains with umbrella covered tables and chairs. One of the dining areas opened to an area on the porch for outside dining.There were large comfortable rocking chairs and end tables along the porch.

After dinner, Sophia and George along with some of the other residents took a stroll throughout the Willowist gardens.Sophia was especially interested in walking by the separate medical research facility but feigned an interest in the gardens so as not to arouse suspicions of the other residents accompanying their walk.For Sophia's benefit George casually noted as they walked near the research facility, "it's for medical research and very secure with guards. We have better things to do than bother with it.It is there on a 99 year lease to the German government, made after WWII. Really, no one pays attention to it. Willowist has a separate assisted living area with health professionals on duty 24/7. That medical research is not used for Willowist residents."

Sophia and George were aware there was an abandoned underground bomb shelter underneath the medical research building which was created during the cold war. Access from the outside was in the wooded area behind the building, and the metal door was covered in grass as it had not been accessed in over fifty years. She had memorized the entire layout of the building from infrared surveillance photos and knew the bomb shelter led to a steel door with access to the basement of the medical research building. Apparently the Germans were unaware of the bomb shelter's existence or didn't bother with it. Anyone looking at the well maintained building, would think it resembled a "charming country retreat."

"All of Willowist had once been a mental institution and retreat for psychiatrists before it was extensively renovated and rebuilt into the posh retirement campus it is today. At one time after WWII, soldiers from various countries with psychological problems were treated at the former setup. No one was sure why Germany leased the medical research facility. Speculation was that a lot of German soldiers were treated at the institution, and Germany began research into post traumatic stress syndrome and made a deal with the United States government to lease the research building for their own use," George continued.

Sophia would discuss the extraction operation with George later, the reason she, George and a third team member were on this assignment. The elderly target of the mission who had once run a concentration camp, would be removed and quietly turned over to German authorities. Which concentration camp or his rank was of no interest to Sophia. One more old, dying Nazi out of the USA and handed off to the German government. The only difference with this operation than the others is that this one was to be done in secret with none of the usual publicity surrounding the capture of a WWII Nazi.

The WWII Nazis were a dying breed but German Chancellor Becker continued to seek them out, and the United States government was happy to cooperate with him and deport any found living in the States.

That was fine with Sophia. It did occur to her that this mission seemed overly complex to extract a single old, dying Nazi. Three team members embedded for several months at a posh resort! "Trying to avoid international attention must involve the Chancellor's own political issues," she considered. She knew the Chancellor was an ally of the United States and had political problems in his own country because he opposed the revival of neo-Nazism. Sophia despised the current trend to glamourize Nazism. But politics are left to others she always believed. She just carried out her orders.

"I know you have been briefed. The renegade paramilitary German High Command often clashes with the Chancellor's global approach and desire to show Germany does not tolerate Nazism. The High Command tries to protect the Nazi's and use them as role models to the young neo-Nazis to ignite their plans to revive the Nazi beliefs," George added. "The High Command treats the Nazi's as though they are victims of the United States and other governments."

"Yes, I know," Sophia replied. "They tortured and murdered thousands of innocent people but they are 'victims'". Her rare sarcasm had an edge to it. Sophia disliked politics and political views.

"They push a conspiracy theory, that the rest of world wants to use the Hitler days to keep Germany politically and militarily weak. Keep the Germans feeling guilty for the actions of the past. Keep Germany from ever becoming a strong military power again. But the rising popularity of the military leader who dislikes Chancellor Becker and espouses neo-Nazism has our government concerned. Too many young Americans are turning to the neo-Nazism movement and Franz Worthermann, the leader of the German High Command has become a powerful counterpoint to the moderate views of Chancellor Becker. Becker wants to put the remaining old Nazis in jail while Worthermann wants to put them on a pedestal. Rehabilitate their image. Make them role models for the neo-Nazi movement," George continued.

While Sophia was on her stroll with George, the intruder opened her apartment door using a master code to the lock and carefully opened dresser drawers, looked in the closet and all around the inside of the apartment. Finding nothing of interest, the intruder quietly left the apartment but with a nagging feeling there was more to Sophia than meets the eye.

When Sophia returned to her apartment, not surprisingly the marker had been moved.Nothing was taken or discovered.Sophia was well-trained and her weapons cache were carefully hidden and secured in benign looking flower boxes on the porch.Every knick knack and picture in the apartment was chosen to confirm Sophia's profile of a retired state department employee as presented to Willowist residents. A picture of her behind an office desk. A thank you desk pencil holder from "state department colleagues." Nothing to disclose her Special Ops training and weapon handling abilities.

CHAPTER 4

Chancellor Becker and Franz Worthermann were childhood friends. Sleepovers, summer camps and vacations together.

"Hey, Becker! Are you in or not?", Worthermann challenged his friend. Worthermann had cornered the kid who made a date with Worthermann's former girl friend. Worthermann was kicking the kid who was on the ground and almost unconscious. "Let him go, Franz. You made your point," Becker replied. Worthermann kept kicking.

As Becker became successful in politics, Worthermann became successful in the German military. So much so, he was feared for his quick temper and unpredictable violent outbursts. Yet the military loved him and many of the German public supported his pro-Nazi views and his intense nationalism. "Germany First, No Apologies" was often the way Worthermann began his public speeches.

Herr Worthermann was raised a Nazi. His family roots went back to the days of Adolf Hitler. His father was a German general who led a successful air assault on the Greek Island of Crete, one of the renowned German victories in WW II. General Worthermann was revered by his soldiers for his bravery and will to win.

Worthermann firmly believed the world needed a return to Nazism with himself as the leader. As he rose to prominence in the military, he became a hero to the neo-Nazi movement.His security forces were as brutal and as ruthless as any of Hitler's SS troops.

Otto Wilhelm's experience helped quell the enthusiasm of those who wanted Worthermann ousted from the military. Wilhelm was a cabinet member who publicly criticized Worthermann repeatedly. One night his wife awoke to a huge man standing by the bed, holding her husband in the air by his throat. The man, known to be Worthermann's top enforcer, Angel, looked her in the eye as he twisted Wilhem's neck and threw the dead body on her. Terrified, she and her children left Berlin to live with family in Spain. Word of Wilhelm's death and of several other anti Worthermann officials spread.

Chancellor Becker was allied with the United States President and suspected Worthermann was planning a terrorist attack there to disrupt American politics and create enough chaos for the Nazis to seize control of the government. And Becker realized Franz Worthermann was in complete control of the German military and was becoming one of the most popular leaders in Germany.

It was Worthermann's popularity that carried Becker into the Chancellorship. But with a price. Becker took orders from Worthermann.

It was 3 a.m. when the sound of broken glass woke up Chancellor Becker's wife Helga, and remembering how her husband trained her, she grabbed her handgun from the night table, and rushed to the children's room. She sat on the bed with her eyes on the door and called her husband.

"Someone is in the house," she whispered excitedly. "I'm in the childrens' room."

"What? We have 24 hour security guards outside," the German Chancellor replied. He was on a tour of a storm ravaged area, 100 miles from Berlin. "Sit tight, I'll get military police there right away."

Helga heard the sounds of footsteps on the stairs and the door open to her bedroom. She aimed the handgun at the door of the children's room. Suddenly it was quiet. No gunshot? She thought she heard someone going down the staircase but wasn't sure enough to leave the room.

About five minutes later her phone rang. "Helga, are you ok? Security should be there any minute."

"We are ok but please come home!"

When the Chancellor returned home several hours later he found his wife sobbing and sitting quietly in the living room, the children asleep on the couch beside her.

"I am sorry, Helga, two of our security guards were strangled and the bodies left outside, the third one disappeared. This is the work of terrorists I am sure."

She looked up at him and hands shaking, she handed him the note that was left by the bedroom door.

"Next time your family dies."

Hysterical, Helga shouted "What did you do! What's going on?"

The Chancellor quietly replied, "Don't worry. Nothing like this will ever happen again."

The Chancellor knew what the warning meant and several days later he promoted his former childhood friend Herr Franz Worthermann as head of the German High Command, in full control of the military.

CHAPTER 5

WILLOWIST

Several weeks went by, and Sophia connected with her other teammate, twenty-eight year old Catina ("call me Cat") Bresset, who was ostensibly at Willowist for an internship on her way to obtaining a Masters in Business Administration degree. Sophia knew, however, Catina was also special ops, had extensive international travel and front line deployment and would be Sophia's other teammate on the extraction mission. She and Cat traded stories on undercover work in Afghanistan when they were sure no one was listening.

Cat grew up north of the Boston area, a working class town called Rockport. Her parents ran a popular tavern visited by tourists as well as locals. Attractive and social, her demeanor belied a tough, smart soldier. The 9/11 World Trade attack angered and distressed her, and she enlisted in the Marines as soon as she was old enough. Revenge on terrorists became her mission.

Cat remembered the tavern going deadly quiet during the terrorist attack on the World Trade Center, and everyone staring at the tv. Just a kid, she couldn't fathom why adults were openly crying. At first she thought the images of airplanes hitting a big tower that caught on fire and started to crumble was a movie. Later her mother quietly explained what happened at the World Trade Center.

"My first real mission was in Iraq," she confided to Sophia. "I was undercover as a nurse to gain access to a hospital there and assassinate a member of Al Qaeda.

"There were several American patients, and I was brought in to help prepare them for the trip home. After they were safely in the hands of a Marine unit, I shot two Iraqi guards outside the door and then shot the terrorist laying in his bed.

"All hell broke loose, and men with high power guns came storming into the hospital, looking for me. I climbed the stairs to the roof and could hear them shouting to each other to not take me alive. A US helicopter appeared as planned, and the crew lowered a rope with a basket and took me to safety.

"And that, Sophia, that was my first mission!"

Cat loved history and especially everything about the music of the 1950's and 60's, and Sophia enjoyed what became afternoon tea discussions, making certain those conversations were overheard by some of the Willowist gossipers, like Esther Chaney. There was less suspicion as to why Sophia and Cat were frequently together.

"Tell me about American Bandstand, Sophia, were you ever on the show?"

"Actually, yes", Sophia laughed. "In eighth grade I won a contest, knew the last name of a singer named Fabian. It was Forte. I was even asked by host Dick Clark to rate a record."

"What song?"

"Turn Me Loose," one of Fabian's first hits. I gave it an 8 out of 10. I was in love with Fabian! Had his picture on my bedroom wall for years! My schoolgirl friends and I always called Fabian and Frankie Avalon 'dreamboats'."

"Did you dance on the show," Cat laughed.

"The Stroll. Bristol Stomp. Jitterbug. Locomotion. Did them all. There was a favorite couple, Justine and Bob, who everyone loved to watch dance.

Neil Sedaka another good old guy. Songs like 'Stairway to Heaven', 'Right Next Door to an Angel' were great songs," Sophia continued.

" I know Stairway to Heaven!,"Cat exclaimed. "The guitar riff at the beginning is awesome."

Sophia laughed, "Listen to the Sedaka version online, it's a little different than the Led Zepplin cover song."

" I have watched old tv shows like The Honeymooners, Leave It To Beaver, and My Three Sons on classic tv. It really was a man's world then," Cat sighed. "But when the biggest problem a family had was that Wally Cleaver gave his high school sweater to a girl and had to ask for it back, those days sound wonderful compared to the drugs and violence today."

Sophia didn't want to disillusion Cat by pointing out the "good old days" weren't so good. Women were abused and given no respect. Families were torn by alcoholism and domestic violence. And people were recovering from WWII while living in fear that a nuclear holocaust blast would come as a result of the Cold War.

Sophia observed, "When I was young there was constant fear all around. Many of my neighbors built underground bomb shelters. The news bombarded us daily with reports of a possible nuclear attack by Russia. Some of the bomb shelters were like underground homes, fully stocked with food, separate ventilation systems, capable of allowing a family to live safely in isolation if a nuclear attack did happen."

"Like the bomb shelter in the German building next store," Cat interrupted.

Pleased that Cat had obviously done her homework for this mission, Sophia replied, "Yep. The early sixties were scary, Cat. Nuclear testing was done in places like Nevada, leading to worldwide fear that the winds would spread fallout carrying strontium-90 released from the nuclear bombs. Strontium-90 if ingested caused bone cancer, and people were terrified of it.

When Jack Kennedy won the election over Richard Nixon for President there was an air of freshness in the country.He and his wife were young, vibrant, exciting role models for us. Optimism began to spread," Sophia continued. "But his resolve and leadership was tested early on in his Presidency.

The Russian leader at the time was Nikita Khrushchev who banged his fist on a table in front of international news reporters saying 'we will bury you', referring to the United States.

President Kennedy was embarrassed after he authorized the Bay of Pigs failed invasion of Cuba. After Castro took control of Cuba and nationalized American businesses there, the rebel leader broke off allegiance to the United States and turned to Russia for support. The plan had been for Cuban counter-revolutionaries exiled to Miami to return to Cuba as an invading force and retake

Cuba from Castro. The land invasion moved forward but Kennedy backed off on promised air support as the international community became aware of the American backed plan, and without air support the invading forces were captured and imprisoned.

Castro became a Cuban hero who stood up to an American plan to invade Cuba. No longer trusting the Chiefs of Staff and military advisors who had pressed him into the invasion plan, Kennedy turned to his own group of advisors.

"Many historians believe the failed Bay of Pigs invasion led President Kennedy to increase military involvement in Vietnam. The President said it was time to 'draw a line in the sand' against communism, and Vietnam was where the United States would be successful."

"The Russian leader Khrushchev again attempted to intimidate Kennedy. I remember watching tv news showing Russian ships steaming toward Cuba carrying nuclear weapons, and President Kennedy ordering a naval blockade of Cuba to stop those ships.

For six days we watched the news in horror as the ships kept coming. It was a dramatic showdown between Kennedy and Khrushchev. At the last moment, Khrushchev backed down and sent the Russian ships home, preventing war between the US and Russia, and reinventing Kennedy's image as Presidential in the eyes of the world. John Kennedy had stared at the Russian leader, and the Russian leader blinked.

It was one of Kennedy's finest moments. Also,he was the one responsible for the Civil Rights Act although Lyndon Johnson took credit for it when he became President after Kennedy was assassinated" Sophia added.

"Oh my, Cat, I am so sorry to be giving you a history lecture. I just got caught up in remembering those days."

" I love it Sophia! You lived through those times, and the history books can't match your personal observations."

It was the terrible reminders of Hitler's genocide that moved Cat emotionally. She had studied the holocaust and had strong feelings against the atrocities committed by the Nazis. Cat's great grandfather, a teacher and member of the Resistance movement against Hitler, had been taken out of his classroom and brutally crucified and murdered by the Nazis. Cat would risk her life to stop anyone connected with Nazism. Exactly why Cat was chosen for the Willowist mission.

"Sophia, it's odd we are imbedded in this luxurious retirement home to extract one old Nazi, even if he had high status. I know many missions take time but this one seems easy enough. We should just smash into the building and take him!"

"We have to follow orders, the politics of it are of no concern to us. There must be political implications. It's not so bad, Cat, living the good life a few months, although when I do retire it will be at a Florida beach community. I like the sun and surf!"

As Sophia and Cat expected, their conversation was of great interest to several of the Willowist residents, especially Rosy DeStefano, a known gossip. DeStefano was a regular in the Gossip Room and was known for her caustic, unflattering remarks about other Willowist residents.

Sophia enjoyed spending time with Cat, who was a confident, strong-willed, well-trained in special ops young woman.

And patriotic.

Sophia was comfortable that Cat was a teammate she could trust with her life.

CHAPTER 6

WILLOWIST

Sophia was startled the first time a man walked by her, looked her in the eye and yelled "Bingo!" and kept walking. She was sitting on the wrap around porch enjoying a spectacular sunset full of colorful pinks, blues and reddish hues

"Bingo Bob" is a recent fixture here, Lady Vikki called over to Sophia. "He randomly calls out Bingo from time to time, whenever the mood hits him. He is a lively, fun man, especially at the Viagra parties."

"Bingo Bob" was Angelo Olivanti, a businessman from New York City. He grew up in New York's Little Italy. Homemade ravioli and other pasta was a staple in the household.His grandmother and his parents were hard-working immigrants. They respected the American culture, were very patriotic and his father was a combat veteran of WW1.

Angelo won a scholarship to Harvard and studied business. Conservative in thought, politics and dress, he planned to return to his family's farming roots in Ascea, Italy. While at Harvard he opened a small store in the

Italian North End of Boston with produce from his family's farm. "Angelo's Organic, Naturally" was a huge hit, and a consortium paid him more money than he could refuse to buy out his business.

While the wealthy families of his Harvard classmates where buying their sons out of being drafted, Angelo volunteered to serve in the Vietnam War after college. Although he had military training in the field, his superiors welcomed his business expertise and moved him out of the paddy fields. He was called upon to review accounting practices of American firms doing business in Southeast Asia. It was near the end of the Vietnam War that Angelo received high security clearances and was hired by federal prosecutors to uncover corruption within the business community's dealing with government contracts. Through Angelo's help, several businesses were targeted by the federal government and their executives sent to federal prisons. Kickbacks to politicians and military leaders for supply of weapons, hiring of politicians families to get contracts. Corruption was rampant during the Vietnam War effort.

SOUTH VIETNAM

In the late 1960's it was a young Angelo's determined effort to "follow the money" that uncovered a scheme among South Vietnamese Army Generals and a high ranking Pentagon official. In a complicated set of transactions the Generals were extorting money from American businesses working in the war effort and funneling kickbacks to the Pentagon official. In return the official used his political influence to keep the Generals in power and supply weapons they could sell. Some of those weapons ended up in the hands of the North Vietnamese and were used against the Generals' own people.

Illegal drugs were flowing from Thailand into South Vietnam on their way into the United States. Angelo became instrumental in identifying the principals involved and disrupting the flow of drugs. Van Thu, a top politician in South Vietnam used thugs, thieves and murderers to run the labs where cocaine was made.

A major problem American soldiers had in Vietnam was distinguishing village people who supported them from village people who were Viet Cong. Angelo helped put together a clandestine operation to infiltrate and destroy the labs in the Vietnam jungle. He insisted on leaving his desk job to participate in the move against the lab.

It was in the Vietnam jungle where Angelo met Al Darrough who was drafted right after college graduation and before law school. His wealthy parents tried to buy his way into the Reserves to avoid Vietnam but Darrough wanted to be in the middle of the fighting. At basic training he and Angelo became close friends and were assigned to the same unit in Vietnam.

Air surveillance had shown the largest lab operating about 40 miles from Saigon. Angelo led an invading team to dismantle the lab. His team trekked through areas controlled by the Viet Cong and moved mostly at night. Mosquitos, leeches, and other disease carrying insects were the least of their worries. Rather, the Viet Cong hid land mines and booby traps made of sharp pieces of bamboo which penetrated into the foot when stepped on, and other such devices that endangered the lives of United States troops.

Robbie Herron was the first of three of Angelo's team to fall victim to the jungle dangers. Only a few miles from Saigon, Robbie screamed in pain as the bamboo spear he stepped on pierced his boots and his foot. The medic on the team couldn't stop the blood, and Robbie died a painful death. Two other team members developed intestinal distress with unstoppable vomiting and diarrhea and were forced to abandon the mission. Angelo prayed no other team member would fall as he anticipated a fight from the soldiers guarding the lab. He was down to nine men plus a medic who was himself dealing with a high fever contracted in the jungle.

Using infrared equipment the team had to navigate even more booby traps the closer they got to the lab. They could see several machine guns strategically placed to defend the lab but they were unmanned. "Not surprising," Angelo whispered to his team. "Who the hell could get close to this jungle lab alive, considering the natural and man-made dangers of this jungle."

Angelo's team cautiously observed the lab operation which was run by a few soldiers working alongside children who looked to be 10 or 12 years old mixing coca leaves with weed eater to make a cocaine paste. There were a few soldiers relaxing smoking joints nearby. While Angelo didn't see any lookouts for the lab, he knew the Vietnamese had an uncanny ability to blend in with the jungle environment. "Just because you can't see them, don't assume they are not there," he cautioned his men.

As dawn broke, Angelo, Al Darrough the rest of his team walked into the lab area firing assault rifles, carbines and throwing grenades indiscriminately. There was some return fire from several guards who had their weapons nearby but the team killed them quickly. Children, soldiers fell without returning fire. Angelo's team had no casualties after the brief shootout with several soldiers. The surprise attack was successful, and only a couple of soldiers not killed ran off into the jungle. The team burned the cocaine material and plodded their way back to friendly forces in Saigon without further incident.

He protested when his superiors ordered him back doing investigations into business operations.He often said to his colleagues "I love the adrenalin rush of military action!" But it was later undercover assignment involving the illegal drug trade of Colombia and money laundering scheme in Panama that put him in more danger than the jungles of South Vietnam.

PANAMA CITY, PANAMA

Shelia Fromme was a millionaire, several times over. Working for a wall street investment firm she had what investors called an "amazing" mind when it comes to money matters. A love affair with a senator who had ties to illegal drug dealing and human trafficking opened the door for her to launder money for the criminal elite. Drug dealers, internet scammers, and other well-heeled criminals hired her to make their illegal money look legally earned.

When Angelo Olivanti was referred to her by one of her clients about "possible investments" by him, she invited him for drinks and dinner at her favorite restaurant MainLine, overlooking Panama Bay. Fromme was a nymphomaniac and liked what she saw in the pictures she had been sent of Angelo. With her black hair, blue eyes and sultry attitude, she often bedded clients, especially married ones to keep them under her thumb through blackmail. She looked at it as insurance if any of them were caught by Interpol. Her clients did not want their families knowing they slept with her.

Before she met Angelo, Shelia Fromme thoroughly investigated him. DEA officials were careful to set up a profile for Angelo about his business and added some information suggesting he was tied to "shady" business deals but left it open that nothing was ever proven. Fromme never met with anyone until she was satisfied they were not undercover or in any way working against her interests.

Angelo was intrigued by her beauty and her ability to stay ahead of law enforcement, considering the extent of her money laundering business which included clients in various countries as Fromme had connections everywhere. And with some nasty people, Angelo mused. He knew the stories of what she had done to people who crossed her. Torture. Murder. Family members murdered. From her sophisticated manner and beauty no one would tie her to violent criminals.

"Hello, Angelo," she said as she extended her hand. Angelo knew immediately he was going to enjoy this assignment. Shelia Fromme looked exciting. Dressed in a black Fendi strap dress, Angelo tried not to stare at her cleavage. "What are you drinking," she asked.

"Scotch, Glenfiddich straight up. Great to meet you, may I call you Shelia?"

"Of course. Waiter! Get my gentlemen friend his drink and hurry it up!" Turning back to Angelo she added "Nice choice. One of my favorite single malts."

After some small talk Angelo followed the script he and his fellow agents developed to entice Fromme into doing business with him.Angelo considered Shelia Fromme may be considered a pushover for sexual escapades but knew she had the ability to manipulate the monetary process, and the always nearby bodyguards showed she is savvy about security.

Angelo hinted he was involved in the illegal drug trade and had to launder money for him and his partners. He told her he was part of a "consortium" that arranged distribution centers across the United States to get the drugs into local communities where demand is high, "especially from young people", he added.

"Your name came up from several different sources as the one to talk to," he said. "They say you can make it all look legal and untouchable from the Feds."

"No doubt about it! Right now you are in a resort purchased with drug money which is 'cleaned' daily. Welcome to our little family of crooks", she laughed.

After a traditional dinner of sancocho followed by ceviche, Fromme said in a whispery voice, "You have interesting deals going on. If you trust me you are going to make a lot of money!"

Fromme smiled, and Angelo felt her foot rubbing his leg. "Why don't we go to my place to finalize the details?"

Angelo didn't get to sit down. Fromme was all over him, kissing him wildly, grabbing at his belt, pulling his pants down. Not one to fight off a beautiful, sexy woman, Angelo picked her up and carried her to the bedroom and began a night of lovemaking that was anything but gentle.

For the next week Angelo cavorted with her in bed, in her private swimming pool, on the counter of her kitchen. On her desk in her lavish office. He laughed to himself that this was an undercover assignment. "How many guys would love to be doing this for work! Getting paid to have sex with a hot woman!" But Angelo knew his mission and what he had to do. He had no interest in a relationship with Fromme. She was beautiful and smart but very dangerous. He had to be careful because there was always at least one bodyguard walking around inside and outside the premises.

At times Fromme seemed uncharacteristically nervous, even unhinged at times, to Angelo. Usually after she received a cell phone. He later learned she had been siphoning funds from a cartel, and she feared her days were numbered. One time after lovemaking she confided to Angelo "I don't know how much time I have anymore. I made some serious mistakes involving some bad people. Make love to me again. I need you."

"I have to go back to New York, Shelia", he pleaded,as she undressed him for another round of lovemaking when she returned from her office. "It's been a blast! We have to do this again."

A week later Angelo contacted her. "We need to meet somewhere private, I am bringing an investor with me, and he doesn't like crowds. "How about that warehouse you showed me outside of Panama City. The one where you store your stuff." He was referring to cocaine and cash.

It was not out of the ordinary for Shelia to meet her clients in deserted places. She kept a handgun in her purse and knew how to use it, "just in case" and was never without at least one bodyguard.

When she arrived at the warehouse with her driver bodyguard, she told him to wait in the car. While Fromme was inside, Angelo's accomplice caught Fromme's driver off guard and choked him until his body went limp.

Something just didn't seem right to Fromm as she walked into the warehouse. She trusted her instincts. One time in Argentina she remembered, a corrupt government official had ordered her murder to steal her contacts and bank accounts.Not trusting the woman, Maria Maz,from the time Fromme first met her, Fromme had beefed up her own security. The night Maz's henchmen broke into Fromme's hotel suite Fromme had taken her usual precaution of sleeping in the spare bedroom and leaving pillows under the covers in the main bedroom. The killers shot the pillows thinking they had Fromme. Before they were able to leave the hotel suite, the would-be murderers were killed by Fromme's bodyguards.

On Fromme's orders the bodyguards went to Maz's house. Maz had completed her usual nightly routine and was sound asleep when she was awakened by two men in her bedroom. "This is from Shelia Fromme" one whispered as they riddled her with bullets.

Fromme's thoughts returned to the present. Did she let her guard down to this good-looking man from the States? Was he there to assassinate her? Was he part of the cartel she had been stealing from? Fromm's instincts kicked in, and she turned to call her bodyguard but he was lying on the ground. Several Panama and Interpol police appeared from behind some boxes, guns drawn. None of them were police who were on her payroll. The Panama contacts of Al Darrough, who was now a top federal prosecutor, made sure Angelo had backup.

Angelo nervously announced to Sheila Fromme that she is being investigated and arrested by Interpol and other law enforcement authorities.

"I am here on behalf of the United States Government. We have detailed information about your involvement in hiding illegal drug money and money from trafficking in children. The United States and Panama governments will offer you protection and a plea deal if you will testify against the Senator and other United States officials involved in the illegal operations. Whatever happens with the Colombian officials involved is of no concern to my government," Angelo announced, somewhat officiously.

"You are going to protect me?"she laughed. "You can't protect me. No one can. They will torture me. They will get the numbers to all the money accounts. Then feed my body to jungle animals.You have no idea about the people involved with me." She didn't mention she had been stealing from the Bandas Cartel.

Without emotion she pulled a gun from her purse, put it in her mouth and pulled the trigger. Shelia Fromme had stolen from the Bandas Cartel and knew this was a much easier way to go. Angelo called Al Darrough from the deserted warehouse where he had a set the meeting with her and described the suicide.

"I'll make a call. It will be cleaned up. Just leave there, never say another word about it, and this will be an event that never happened. Officially, Shelia Fromme will have disappeared. Absconded with illegal drug money. Vanished," Darrough promised. "Stay on the case."

Angelo took Fromme's house keys from her purse. Arriving at the house he and his Panama police agent counted several bodyguards. "How many?" "There are three outside, let's take them out and hope none inside", the Panama contact suggested. Angelo shot out the security cameras and hit one of Fromme's men but the other two fired back.

The Panama police agent was hit, and the men retreated into the house. Angelo had to wait for backup, and then several police stormed the house with him. Shots were fired indiscriminately from both sides, and Fromme's men as well as two police officers were killed.

"Fromme was living the good life," Angelo noted as he saw expensive artwork and furniture throughout. The house was deserted, and they took their time searching for information. Surprisingly, Fromme had left her laptop on a desk in her bedroom, not secure in a safe.

He removed the flash drive and laptop, which later his tech friend would hack into. It was filled with information about the money laundering schemes, including implicating the senator and other public officials involved in corruption with her.

CALI, COLOMBIA

In Cali, El Gringo threw his laptop on the ground. "Fuck! Somebody wiped out one of my accounts

Fromme set up. Millions gone!" He ordered Malachi to take some men and "find that bitch".

When Malachi arrived he approached the house cautiously. Satisfied there was no activity he and the men searched the house, even tearing open some wall areas looking for secret panels. "No sign of Fromme, Boss. Looks like she abandoned the property. There is nothing here."

"Blow up the house! I will track her down and tear her apart myself ," El Gringo shouted into the phone. "And find me that goddamn Angelo Olivanti. From what I heard, he was fucking her and may have taken off with her and my money."

NEW YORK CITY

The atmosphere at the Castaway Bar, club members only, of the Hotel Lord in New York City was sophisticated and subdued. More wall street million dollar deals were consummated here than anywhere else in Manhattan. An expensive Monet painting was behind the bar, tables and booths surrounded by various planters, assuring privacy for the patrons. Tourists who ventured in were courteously steered into the Regent Tavern a few steps away by Gustavo, the gracious but firm maitre'd. "Have a drink in the Tavern room on me," as he led the tourists away from the Castaway Bar. "Can't these people read," he muttered as he looked at the nondescript door leading to the Castaway Bar which was clearly labeled "Members Only."

"I have it!," Angelo excitedly mentioned to Al Darrough as Darrough settled into the booth with him. "Johnnie Walker Blue Label," Darrough said to the waiter. "What the hell, Angie, don't look at me that way, the taxpayers don't give a shit what I drink as long as I get results."

Angelo gave him the flash drive with the results of all of Shelia Fromme's money laundering scheme. "Al, I want to be kept out of this. You promised. These players are nasty, ruthless. It's El Gringo again! You put him away once with my research and protected my identity. But he escaped from jail and is back in the business. I want nothing, absolutely nothing to do with exposing his latest criminal enterprise. Even a year later I still have nightmares about him coming after me!"

El Gringo had been moving tons of cocaine into a Miami port with the help of a shipping company that imported coffee and other staples from Colombia. Cocaine was carefully loaded into the bottom of coffee containers and covered over with coffee beans. Most of the cargo was inspected by some officials on El Gringo's payroll but even the honest ones never uncovered the illegal drugs.

Angelo had been assigned to review accounting practices of various shipping companies and discovered several shell companies eventually leading to the one owned by the Bandas cartel. His research led to charges being filed against El Gringo, who was jailed despite the corruption in the Colombian legal system.

Darrough clinked his $800 glass of scotch paid for by taxpayer money in a toast with Angelo's sparkling water. "This Senator is going down! And I am in the mix for Vice-President in the next election. This case will do it for me, you will be in my cabinet. Tomorrow I will get you some security until this is all over."

Angelo summarized how the Senator used his influence to arrange for Miami ports to be used for the delivery of illegal drugs and even trafficking young girls. "This guy should be hung," he thought. "Kids, drugs. Sickening."

Neither men noticed they were being watched closely by a man in a nearby booth who had slipped Gustavo ten one-hundred dollar bills to be seated there. The man was texting with someone.Angelo and Darrough joked about being found hanging from a bridge in Cali if the Bandas members knew arrests were coming their way.

Darrough left first to return to his office and start the arrest process. "I want to be the lead on the national news!" Darrough said as he left the table.

The lead on the national news later that day reported "Top Federal Prosecutor Al Darrough found dead of an apparent suicide." Had anyone other than federal agents who responded to the scene, it would be clear Al Darrough did not commit suicide. His mouth was covered with tape, his hands were bound, and there were deep cuts on his face and arms. Not wanting to create a major media event, the feds spread the false story that a depressed Al Darrough took his own life. The suicide story would lose interest much quicker than if the media reported Darrough was murdered by a drug cartel ties to corrupt government officials.

Interestingly, the Fromme information on El Gringo disappeared along with the detective who had custody of it.

The two men waiting for him in his apartment poured themselves a drink and sat at Angleo's dinner table. They were not surprised that Angelo Olivanti never returned to his apartment. Shaken, concerned for his safety, Angelo quickly disappeared into the Witness Protection Program of the United States government. Not even his family knew where he ended up. Ever the marketing genius, Angelo reinvented himself as Bingo Bob O'Donnell and joined the Willowist retirement community. A brand new man!

CHAPTER 7

CALI, COLOMBIA

El Gringo had been arrested on information supplied from Angelo Olivanti, who uncovered the ties between his drug operation in Colombia and the deliveries of cocaine at Miami port. United States attempts to extradite him were denied by corrupt prosecutors, judges and Colombian officials. After he was convicted and sentenced to fifteen years in jail, he boasted to his lawyer "I'll be out before you know it." Then he added, "you are a fucking lousy lawyer. The judge and jury were paid, and you still lost the case."

A week later his lawyer was walking to his car in the office building garage, and a car with four males pulled up alongside him. "Do you know where we can get some good Colombian coffee?", the driver asked. The lawyer saw the gun in his hand and ran toward his car, screaming "help me, help me!" A moment later a hail of gunfire came from the car, and the lawyer collapsed to the ground, dead. "El Gringo sends his regards," the driver shouted as the car sped away.

During the time El Gringo was in the Colombian jail there was no doubt who was the Top Dog. El

Gringo's cell looked like a small apartment. A leather lounge chair, microwave, refrigerator, desk, computer and internet were neatly placeD throughout the cell. Dinners were catered. He had full use of a satellite phone, and his cell door was never locked.

"What do you mean we lost some neighborhoods to that idiot!', he shouted into the phone. "Just because I am in the goddamn jail doesn't mean Latril can take over my streets!"

Latril was a small time cartel drug leader who decided to expand when El Gringo was arrested. His men shot El Gringo's street dealers in one of the Cali neighborhoods, and El Gringo was livid. Latril, like so many other young boys, was recruited as a low level dealer in a regional cartel careful not to compete with the larger Bandas cartel.

His street smarts and ambition aided his upward movement in the organization. Not afraid to rob, kidnap and murder, he became the right hand man to the cartel leader. Alone with the leader one night Latril sliced his throat and planted fake information on him implicating the leader as a snitch. From that moment on Latril took over the smaller regional cartel and when El Gringo went to jail, Latril made moves to infiltrate the Bandas cartel.

"Take them out. Now!" El Gringo decided the truce with Latril was over. That evening Latril was having dinner with his family, and he noticed it was uneasily quiet outside. As he stood up from the table the door burst open, and Latril, his wife and two teenage children were shot to death. His bodyguards' bodies were found outside. The official police report was Latril killed his family, then himself. The newspapers didn't even mention the deaths. Reporters who got too involved in stories on the drug wars were murdered. Besides, Latril's death was just another death as usual in the drug world.

It was less than a year of his jail sentence when the two evening corrections officers in charge of El Gringo took the night off at the same time because of "family emergencies." The two substitutes gave El Gringo a uniform similar to theirs, and the three of them walked out of jail. Although his escape prompted a federal investigation into the prison superintendent and guards, nothing came of it.

Several days later El Gringo stood calmly in the middle of the street, took aim, pulled the trigger on the Uzi, and the four street dealers fell over. "They wanted war, they got war," he bellowed. "No one sells drugs in Cali or anywhere in Colombia without my permission!" El Gringo made no attempt to carry out assassinations in private. If anything, he wanted his enemies to know he feared no one and that he controlled politicians, police and businessmen.

The phone rang in a high level Colombian government office. "Hey, what's up," El Gringo asked of the cabinet member he controlled. "Where did your dumbass President set up police checkpoints so I know what neighborhoods to avoid."

"Don't call me during work hours, please!", the cabinet member in the Colombian government replied. " Isn't it enough I helped you escape from jail? There are some in this Administration that don't trust me as it is."

"Hahaha, who would trust an idiot like you," El Gringo laughed. "I don't give you all that money for you to live the good life without getting something in return.

I will call you anytime I want. Now where the fuck are those checkpoints."

"I'll send the coordinates to your phone." The cabinet member knew not to push El Gringo or he would end up like his predecessor with his head in a box delivered to the President.

Even the normally aggressive news reporters avoided mentioning El Gringo on the news. Too many reporters had been murdered in the last two years. The drug war was winding down thanks to El Gringo taking control.

Another of El Gringo's distributors had tried to take over the cartel, which led to shootouts in Cali streets. Roscoe Red's men shot and killed El Gringo's street dealers and replaced them with people loyal to him. When Roscoe's dismembered body was found hanging from a Cali bridge, suddenly the street dealer shootings stopped and that was the last of challengers to El Gringo.

The druglord ordered his bodyguards to return to his safe house. He poured a glass of aguardiente and considered his success. His return to the control of drugs in Cali was complete. After six bloody weeks of eliminating competitors, El Gringo was in total control of the illegal drug business. His time in prison had caused fractures in his cocaine cartel but his current reign of fear served its purpose, he was in charge again. "The spoiled gringo kids in Miami, Philadelphia and Los Angeles can get high again," he said to no one in particular. El Gringo prided himself on top quality cocaine and an efficient distribution organization, which faltered somewhat when he was in prison. The Bandas Cartel was number one again.

He turned his attention to his ongoing search for Angelo Olivanti. One person he personally wanted to make"pushing daises".

"Any news? What the hell am I paying you idiots for," El Gringo screamed into the satellite phone. "You DEA agents on my payroll are useless! Find out where Olivanti is and do it now, he cost me millions when he and Darrough put me in prison. Olivanti will be pushing daises like Darrough as soon as I find him.

The news on Darrough's death didn't make the news in Cali. There were assassinations of local leaders that weren't reported. One more gringo lawman murdered was of no concern in Cali.

"Give me time, it's not easy to get information on the Witness Protection Program. We at least got rid of Darrough for you," agent Billy Green carefully replied as El Gringo slammed the phone down. Billy Green was on the take, he and a few rogue agents were on the payroll of the Bandas Cartel, and now the pressure was on for him to deliver Angelo to the druglords so they could exact their revenge. El Gringo had a temper and was not known for his patience. Green knew he had to find Olivanti and find him fast.

MIAMI

Billy Green led the inspection of several cargo ships that arrived from Cali, Colombia. The usual entries into the United States. Coffee. Fruit. Nuts. Cocaine.

Green and his agents paid customs officials well, and the shipments were always easily cleared. He remembered his first meeting with El Gringo in Colombia. Green was sent to investigate the murder of several DEA agents, and the Colombian druglord was the prime suspect. His pilot, unknown to Green, was on El Gringo's payroll and landed the plane on a private airstrip in the Colombian mountains where the plane was surrounded by armed men.

Green was searched, a hood put over his head, and he was delivered to an outpost in the jungle. It was a fully functioning cocaine lab protected by a group of heavily armed guards. He was led into a tent, and when his hood was removed he was facing El Gringo, the single most feared druglord in Colombia.

"How about an aguardiente with me," El Gringo offered.

Slightly shaken, fearfully, Billy Green had a drink with the druglord.

"We can do this one of two ways, you can be buried here in the jungle or you can make a lot of money working with me. I know you have a gambling problem and if your superiors find out, you will be out of the DEA. Those bad people you owe money will not bother you anymore, that is guaranteed. I need a good agent to help the Miami deliveries. Every time there is an election some politician gets all full of himself about saying no to drugs and shutting down the cartels. But all the gringos don't stop enjoying Colombian cocaine. Much more than they do our coffee," he laughed. "What do you say?"

Green didn't hesitate to join what he later called "the cocaine club" and enlisted several fellow agents into the criminal enterprise. He quickly became El Gringo's go-to man not only in South Florida but also up and down the eastern seaboard.

Billy Green always wanted to work in drug enforcement but for the wrong reasons. He saw being a federal agent as a way to become rich. He grew up in a tough neighborhood in Queens and while he avoided gangs, he saw how they intimidated neighborhood mom and pop stores for protection money. And he saw how a few corrupt police let it happen. Once he was in the DEA he reached out to the Bandas cartel and offered his services.

He remembered his first meeting with El Gringo where he was taken with a hood over his head over jungle terrain to an encampment in the Colombian jungle. Seated on a bench with the hood still over his head, El Gringo asked "Why should I trust you? Tell me right now why I shouldn't put a bullet in your head."

Billy Green answered, "We can both make a lot of money. I can help you move product. I can help you with your business." "Kill him," El Gringo said to his guards, testing Green's reaction. Green remained calmed and simply responded "Your loss." Impressed with Billy Green's coolness, the druglord said "You are a badass. But if you fuck with me, you and your family will be dead." From that moment on Billy Green was on the payroll of the Bandas Cartel and expected to help them export drugs into the United States.

Green's superiors in the DEA suspected there was a snitch in the operatives assigned to Colombia but no one suspected him. As Green often said to his colleagues in DEA, "the flow of illegal drugs is not our fault. Our President demands open borders, and illegal drugs, weapons, human trafficking is flourishing. Criminals from all over the world are entering the United States through Mexico." He thought be didn't add "and Miami."

Anytime the DEA had plans to intercept Colombian ships on suspicion of drugs, Green texted El Gringo, and the ships diverted their course. When customs searched the ships upon entry to the Miami port, Green helped make sure the ships carrying illegal cargo were searched by people on El Gringo's payroll, finding nothing but excellent Colombian coffee beans.

The demand for cocaine was high in the States, and Green was paid well by the cartel for the users to m get their product. He personally oversaw millions of dollars of illegal drugs entering the United States.

Billy Green was rich, but now knew his ability to enjoy being alive and spending that money was dependent on finding the whereabouts of Angelo Olivanti.

WILLOWIST

At Willowist, Angelo Olivanti, now in the Witness Protection Program had reinvented himself as Bingo Bob O'Donnell, where he was known as a "dandy."Three piece vested suits, carefully tied bowtie and well manicured black hair sprinkled with gray, the ladies gravitated to Bingo Bob. They found his occasional shouts of "Bingo" to be endearing. Bingo Bob was a fun man to be around. Deadpan sense of humor, the ladies compared him to Bob Newhart. Always ready with a humorous anecdote, Bingo Bob was a favorite at Willowist.

Bob was a runner, like Sophia. In the early morning hours he would do a couple of miles around the Willowist gym indoor track and often ran alongside Sophia. They became friendly, and the gossip ladies couldn't decide if Bingo Bob and Sophia were a couple or if George and Sophia were a couple. Or if they were a threesome, gossip Esther Chaney once giggled to her friends.

Bob loved gossip. "Do you believe the sweater Becky has on?" "Looks like Mary had implants." "Millie's hairstyle is so 50's." The ladies loved his lighthearted observations and sense of humor. Bingo Bob was one of the few men at Willowist who dared to venture into the Gossip Room.

Like Sophia, Bob was in excellent physical shape for his age. Careful about his diet, he often talked to the kitchen crew about more healthy choices for the residents. But Bingo Bob never questioned or tried to change the Philly cheesesteak recipes of the Swoop Sisters. Some things were sacred, he laughed to himself. An organic Philly cheesesteak was an impossibility he told the chefs.

Bob and Sophia occasionally sat together on one of the garden benches and discussed the 1960's. Both agreed the violent protests that swept the country in the summer of '66 were "un-American." Both agreed in the importance of a strong military. Both agreed most young people today did not understand the sacrifices their grandfathers and great grandfathers made for them in fighting the Nazis and Adolf Hitler's world domination plan.

Bob introduced Sophia to the Swoops, and Sophia immediately hit it off with the sisters. Elizabeth Mary ("Lizzie") and Mary Margret Murphy grew up in an Irish household in the Italian area of South Philadelphia with a family completely devoted to Philadelphia Eagles football.

The "Swoop Sisters" were nicknamed after the Eagles mascot and installed several huge flat screen televisions in a large community room which Willowist provided to the Swoops during football season. Every game day featured homemade Philly cheesesteaks, other snacks and a full bar. Crestor and Pepto Bismol were available as needed.

Sundays were fun days for the sports minded Willowist residents, and there were lots of them. Because there were three women to every man at Willowist, and the men followed football, the ladies were football fans.

At first glance, the Sisters looked like twins, although Elizabeth ("Lizzy") was two years older than Mary Margret. Slightly pudgy and each about 5'2, the sisters didn't just laugh, they howled. An infectious, sustained, loud howl that when started spread to anyone within earshot.

The Sisters had worked in a garment factory until the imports forced severe cutbacks and eventually the closure of most of the industry. With their savings and no experience in the restaurant business, Lizzy and Mary Margaret opened a catering business which led to a small café which led to a successful sports bar frequented by the most intense and rabid Eagles fans in South Philly. The boys from the 'hood loved going to the Swoop Sisters SportsBar. And it didn't hurt business that Eagles players often stopped by.

A restaurant chain bought out the Sisters and gave them the opportunity to retire, ending up at Willowist. Without the sisters' personality, the SportsBar became just that, an average, run of the mill chain-restaurant tavern. But Willowist gained two entertaining, lovable residents.

The Swoops were close friends with the Eagles owners and were given two connecting luxury box suites for every home game. The suites were on a level with only one other suite, on the other side of the scoreboard. Willowist residents would sign up in advance and join the

Swoops for the games. This year was special because the Eagles were playing the New York Jets and were home field favorites to win the Super Bowl. This was the first time in Super Bowl history the game was being played at the home field of one of the teams in the Super Bowl. Eagles fans were ecstatic.

With their South Philadelphia accent, hearty laugh and vibrant personalities, the Sisters were loved by all at Willowist. Even the critics in the Gossip Room had nothing derogatory to say about the Swoops.

CHAPTER 8

WILLOWIST

Willowist was a sprawling campus, acres of willow trees, hill and valley areas sprinkled with colorful wild flowers and walking trails, gardens with meticulous landscaping.

Elevators were strategically placed for the convenience of the residents. Electric carts with baskets, similar to those found in grocery stores, were readily available to navigate the interconnected hallways throughout all four stucco buildings as well as to all the common areas.

Each apartment had a living room, master bedroom and bath, guest bedroom and bath and kitchen area. Daily maid service for those who desired it, smart tv's, gas fireplaces. Although every resident was given a laptop and cell phone, each apartment also had a landline with speed dials to the various Willowist services.

Unknown to the residents, however, the courtesy laptop and cell phone provided to every resident was programmed with spyware so that the administrator of Willowist, Hans Hansberger, could access their private browsing, emails, contact, calls and other uses of the internet whenever he wished. Hans rarely accessed the information because he hated the elderly residents, and all of their discussions were gossip or dining or show reservations.

The tech knowledge gave George the means to hack into Hans' system. He occasionally listened in to conversations of the residents and his eye twitched every time some lady talked about him. Sophia, Cat and he had secure wifi and satellite phones and only used the Willowist devices for routine reservations.

George remembered the conversation between Viola Lepere and Rosy DeStefanao. "That new resident, George, he's a real looker!" Just that statement made George's eye twitch. But it was the mention of Alma Woodruff that got his attention. "Too bad Alma has declared him her territory," Rosy continued. "Wait until he finds out she is a mental case. And violent!". George didn't like the sound of that.

George had a mini tech room set up in his spare bedroom. Whenever he left his apartment he hid the laptop and monitor behind bath towels in the bathroom closet. He purposely locked his apartment closet to draw attention there even though there was nothing in there that would expose his undercover role.Even if an intruder got their hands on his laptop, any failed attempts to access the information would automatically delete it from the hard drive but stored it safely on his secure cloud site. His two drones were carefully hidden in the wooded area, ready to be called up instantly on his computer.

The campus had a concert hall, several indoor and outdoor swimming pools, fitness and yoga center, variety of restaurants, cafes and even several health food grocery stores were designed, as the brochure stated "to provide residents with a healthy lifestyle in their golden years."

There were lectures by authors, artists and chefs. Other than the bus trips offered for theatres and shopping in the New York City, there was no need for anyone to leave the campus. When Engelbert Humperdinck or Tom Jones gave a show at Willowist, Hans had to assign extra paramedics to treat the elderly female residents who fainted or hyperventilated. The sight of 70 year old women throwing bras and panties on the stage gave Hans nightmares. Hans banned Richard Simmons, the aerobics guru after several residents needed medical attention after trying to emulate his moves.

Overall, the living experience at Willowist soothed the aches, pains and fears of old age.Exclusive, expensive, luxurious.

There was a connected assisted living wing where Willowist residents who needed regular home health care stayed. Here there were nurses stations and all the medical equipment needed to care for the Willowist seriously or even terminally ill. It was a mini-hospital and hospice.

There was a separate medical research building on a 99 year lease to the German government. It had diplomatic status, meaning the United States government had no control over it. Willowist residents paid no attention to it, and it was card access only, even Hans was excluded from entry. Sophia, Cat and George's mission was to gain entry to that building and remove the WWII Nazi war criminal being kept alive there.

Two stories high and architecturally consistent with the Willowist building, it was surrounded by gardens and protected by an alarm system with security cameras. A parking lot for seven or eight cars led to a path connecting the parking lot with the main gate entrance. There was a rear entrance for deliveries accessed from the parking lot by a dirt road partially hidden by the wooded area on the side of the building opposite Willowist. The medical research building was attractive, environmentally sound and highly secure. There was a private airfield about a mile away for use by the Germans, with a path through the woods to the building by use of ATV's.

Inside, the front half of the first floor was a large office area, with about ten individual cubicles. A staff member at each cubicle had a state-of-the-art desktop computer, tied into a secure wireless internet. The rear half of the building was configured as private living quarters for the researchers. In addition to the individual bedrooms, there was a recreational lounge area and a kitchen area with a full time cook. Although all spoke English, German was the language of choice within the research facility, except when there was an occasional visitor.

There was no medical research going on in the medical research building. It was an active neo-Nazi control center where the Germans committed to a return of the Third Reich could maintain communications with Nazi cells all over the world and report back to one man, Franz Worthermann, head of the German High Command.

Access to the second floor was unobtrusive and by one elevator with stairs next to it. Security cameras kept a watchful eye on each of the two floors, and there was an armed security guard where the elevator opened to the second floor.

On the second floor there was only one patient, kept alive by medical equipment supervised by a doctor and a nurse. It was that patient Sophia and her team planned on extracting. An elderly former high-ranking Nazi who had been in charge of a concentration camp. Sophia knew they had to remove that Nazi before Franz Worthermann carried out his plan for an uprising by neo-Nazi supporters.

CHAPTER 9

HAMBURG, GERMANY

Herr Worthermann banged is hand on the desk, startling the other High Command members in the room. "Why is that American college student still writing news articles about me, Deputy Chief Corporal Amsel?"

Amsel was a loyal Worthermann supporter and with his bodyguard Angel Sebast often carried out the unpleasant violent responses to critics of Herr Worthermann. Worthermann was referring to recent news articles implying the High Command had ties to neo-Nazi groups. Several of the articles had the byline "Chrissy Rice, American student."

Worthermann didn't take kindly to criticism. One of Chancellor Becker's consultants tried to prevent Worthermann from being named leader of the German High Command. The offender was leaving his office late one night, alone, when he was forcefully taken into a waiting car. Dead of a brutal strangling by Worthermann's enforcer Angel Sebast, the consultant's body was dumped in a seedy area of the city, known for illicit sex parlors and random muggings, to make it look as though the death had nothing to do with any political moves against Franz Worthermann.

Amsel and Angel were in charge of kidnapping, torturing, and murdering perceived enemies of the neo-Nazis. Both were feared by allies of Worthermann as well as by enemies. By any definition, Amsel and his sidekick were sociopaths.

"I am confused Boss. What are we supposed to do with her?" Angel asked. His demeanor was subservient and quiet when talking to Worthermann.

"Moron!" When Worthermann was agitated it seemed like the scar on his left cheek turned bright red. His father demanded perfection, and once when Worthermann came home from school with a less than perfect report card, the beating he took was more brutal than the usual beatings his father inflicted. Even now, staring at Amsel, the pain of the sharp knife his father scraped across his young face ached as though it was just happening.

Worthermann always had sought his father's approval. His family was committed to the Third Reich, Worthermann grew up hating Jews, Catholics and everyone else except full bloodied Germans. The Master Race, in his mind.

He studied military history from the Prussian Empire to the present and believed that people wanted to be told how to think, act and behave by their government. Worthermann was intolerant to different opinions and did not hesitate to use violence to accomplish his aims.

Although German authorities investigated, the circumstances surrounding his mother's death from an overdose of sleeping medication was never determined.

Accident? Suicide? Murder? Worthermann suspected his father murdered his mother because he had seen and heard his father physically assault her for reasons as minor as serving him lukewarm coffee."She obviously deserved it" Worthermann thought, giving his father the benefit of the doubt.

Worthermann feared his father but also idolized him. Hitler's portrait was front and center over their fireplace, and every morning Worthermann and his father would salute the picture before Worthermann left for school. The collapse of the Nazi regime upset a young Franz Worthermann, and he vowed bring back the Third Reich.

"Let me think. Let me think. We can't hurt her or make her disappear. Just make sure that bitch Rice is kept under surveillance, The last thing we need to do is give Becker and that jackal of an American President an opportunity to investigate us. Let's find out her weakness and use it against her," he growled at Angel.

CHAPTER 10

BERLIN

Chrissy Rice grew up in Newport Beach, California where the surfing world was part of her life almost from birth. She was an outstanding surfer in high school and was being groomed for a national surfing competition and lucrative magazine deals. But her athletic career ended abruptly that summer.

She and her friends were treading water awaiting a good surfing wave when she felt something brush against her. A few seconds later she felt it again. Horrified, she saw blood coming from out of the water and felt sharp pains her leg. Her friend closet to her in the water screamed "shark! shark!" and Chrissy, screaming in pain, paddled her way to the beach where a lifeguard gave her first aid. Several operations of reconstructive surgery saved her ability to walk but Chrissy's surfing days were over.

Not the best student in high school, she decided to take German to satisfy a foreign language credit. The students considered the German teacher a lot easier in grading than the Spanish teacher and the German language classes filled up quickly. Chrissy set her sights on journalism and was accepted into a semester abroad program in Germany.Before her trip abroad, she studied the present day German government structure and background of German leaders. Chrissy was pleased to learn of the cordial relationship Chancellor Becker had with the American President. "Cooperation instead of confrontation" her German teacher had lectured.

Chrissy remembered her feelings of helplessness and frustration at not being able to have a career in the surfing world. She focused on her studies and envisioned becoming a sought after journalist. Maybe even covering the sport of surfing! Her thoughts drifted back to the present in her college class in Germany just in time to hear the professor call her name."Miss Rice, do you think the neo-Nazi movement has any support in the United States?" The class was studying the rebirth of Nazism, and she had just received a research assignment on the subject.

Aware the German students' eyes were on her, she answered carefully. "I think there are pockets of extremism for many political and religious causes in the United States. We have an open democracy, tolerant of diversity."

"Neo-Nazism, then, is an example of extremism, in your opinion?" The professor stayed on her.

"Extremism is subjective. I do think people who support neo-Nazism are entitled to their opinion." "But," she added, "I think they don't have an understanding of history and the awful reign of terror of Adolf Hitler."

Fortunately for Chrissy the bell ending class rang as her additional comment brought some nasty looks from other students.

A few days later she returned from class to see a swastika painted on her apartment door but she resolved to concentrate on her studies and continue working on her research paper. Chrissy kept hearing the name of Franz Worthermann and became interested in learning more about this current day Nazi leader.

Chrissy spent hours on the internet and in the town library researching the rise of Adolph Hitler and how he enticed German youth into becoming his followers. She was visibly shaken when she read that the Hitler boys youth group from ages 14 to 18 were trained in paramilitary activities and that even younger boys and girls were recruited into Nazi youth groups.

"This is frightening to think all this is starting again," she said to herself.

Chrissy mentioned her research project while sharing some weed with classmates in a late night political discussion and was alarmed at the reaction of her friends, especially those from the United States.

"I would join one of those groups in a second." "Too many minorities are making demands and demand entitlement to whatever they want." "Fuck the losers in government, Heil Hitler, I wish he were alive."

Emboldened and distressed by her friends' surprising support for the neo-Nazi movement, Chrissy decided to dig into neo-Nazism and offer her research paper to the editor at DIE ZIN, the newspaper where she was an intern, despite her professor's warning "you don't know what you are getting yourself into."

The editor at the paper did not fear reprisals from Worthermann. She had the protection of the Chancellor and wanted to see an end to Worthermann and his plans to bring back Nazism. Elisa Otto had family members who had been tortured and died in concentration camps.

"Just make sure your facts are correct, and I will publish a series as you write the columns" she had told Chrissy. A couple of articles had already come out which put Worthermann in an unflattering light.

"Who is Franz Worthermann? the headline of the first article screamed. Chrissy's article was a bio of Worthermann with hints of his ties to the neo-Nazi movement but no real conclusions. The attention the article received from the barrage of phone calls, emails and even some threats to "blow up the news building", showed Elisa and the reporters the intense interest by the German public. Political opinion was split, the country was divided. Worthermann had enemies but also had popular support, which worried Chancellor Becker.

Chrissy Rice was determined to keep writing about Franz Worthermann.

CHAPTER 11

WILLOWIST

The Gossip Room, as it was known, was a tastefully decorated tea room, open for lunch and afternoon delicacies, facing one of Willowist's many gardens.Expensive Ursula red booths along the walls, with a row of red tables for two in the middle of the room and oil paintings, hanging plants, soft Mozart and chamber music in background. A full wet bar to service residents with afternoon cocktails and pre-dinner Happy Hour drinks completed the ambience and amenities of the Gossip Room.

This is where rumors started and flowed through Willowist. Relationships, clothes, bank accounts were all whispered about whomever wasn't present at the moment. "Can you believe how Eleanor is flirting with Ed?" "Where did Esther get that awful jacket?"

Viola Lepere and her three best friends, Rosemary DeStefano, Suzy Petuch and Esther Chaney, mockingly know as the "Crew" were the nastiest of nasty. Other women residents feared their sarcasm and demeaning comments. Comments on hair, make-up, dress, nothing was sacred.

Sophia was the subject of the moment as the Crew shared a second bottle of merlot.

She hooked up with George pretty fast," Rosemary DeStefano complained. "I thought I was getting somewhere with him."

"What? You sit down next to him at dinner uninvited and you think he's in love with you," Suzy Petuch snapped.

"I was working him." Rosemary took a sip of her merlot.

"Well, you're not now. They dine together, take walks together and who knows what goes on in the bedroom."

"Shut up, Suzy", Rosemary hissed. "Sophia comes across classy and nice but I don't like her. And did you see the way Eleanor was flirting with Dr. Sam?"

"Rosemary. Dr. Sam is deaf, 84 years old and doesn't go to the monthly Viagra Night dinner for the men. She won't get any of anything," Suzy responded.

"There's always money!"

"Yes, and we are all too old to spend it."

"But he's a *doctor!* A good catch!", added Esther.

"I don't like Sophia," Rosemary sniffed. The Crew reluctantly agreed Sophia was well-liked by the other guests, especially the Swoop Sisters, and the men flocked to be around her. Social, but not talkative about herself, Sophia avoided being included in any of the cliques that inevitably develop in a retirement community like Willowist.

Esther Chaney announced. "I don't like her either", referring to Viola's obvious antagonism toward Sophia.

Viola sat quietly, thinking back to high school prom night. How she and her senior year sweetheart, Scotty

Townsend, got into an argument at a party. Scotty, very drunk on Iron City Beer, admitted to Viola his love for Sophia. Scotty and Sophia had briefly dated during their freshman year but Sophia broke it off after Scotty cheated on her with "that whore Marianne Winters."Besides, Sophia was not ready to develop a personal relationship knowing full well her future plans had precedence over any romance. Scotty never got over the break-up, even after he and Viola became a couple. Viola remained jealous of Scotty's desires to have a relationship with Sophia.

The party was at Crestwood's, an onsite catering business whose owners allowed illegal underage drinking and partying. Drugs were officially banned but the smell of marijuana permeated the room.

Sophia was the "IT" girl, and many of the boys wanted one last chance to date her before graduation but she kept her distance from all of them. She even refused Scotty's several attempts at a slow dance with her as Viola glared her way. Scotty was drinking beer and taking shots of whiskey when he slurred to Viola "I am winning Sophia back. You'll see." As he staggered across the dance floor toward Sophia, he stumbled. Sophia steadied him, and he pleaded with her to "get back together. We belong together."

Viola, suppressing a cry, began wildly kissing a surprised Jonathan Ferry, who was standing nearby and who decided to enjoy the moment and kissed her back. Sophia, ready to leave, was worried about leaving a drunken Scotty at the party and offered to drive him to his home.

Later, Viola would reflect as to why did Sophia drive Scotty home from the party? Yes, he was drunk. Yes, he and Viola had a heated argument. "You are flirting with Sophia again", Viola had accused him. But if Sophia had let Viola and Scotty work out their problems, Scotty would be alive. The driver going through a red light and smashing into Sophia's car would have hit someone else. Some other passenger in some other car would be dead not Scotty. Sophia escaped with some cuts and bruises but "Sophia should have been the one to die", Viola thought to herself.

And now, after all these years, at a time Viola should be enjoying her retirement, Sophia is back into her life. Somehow, someway, its payback time for Sophia, Viola promised herself.

Viola's thoughts came back to the present.

"Well, girls, I have things to do, see you at dinner."

Suzy finished her strawberry pie and left for her afternoon massage.

"Don't you think Suzy is putting on some poundage?", Rosemary said to a friend at the next table. "And Viola is looking a little pale."

It was never good to be one of the early ones to leave the Gossip Room.

CHAPTER 12

WILLOWIST

Hans Hansberger was in his sixth month Willowist administrator, appointed directly by his political ally, the German Chancellor. A professional marketer with a knack for smiles and handshakes, he was chosen to run Willowist with all its amenities as a reward for the support and money he raised for the Chancellor's election. It was a choice assignment in the States, not quite an ambassadorship, but a position many had wanted.

Hans thought about Tilly.It wasn't that long ago he met Tilly Miller at a seminar in Germany. They ended up together in a cab from the airport to the hotel and never left one another's company for the entire three day workshop. Her gentle caresses turned into wild lovemaking had exhausted him with pleasure.

Hans had security clearances from the German government thanks to his ties with Chancellor Becker and was a top tier bureaucrat but Tilly was evasive on her exact occupation. Hans didn't care about her job, he was enthralled at her beauty, intelligence and lovemaking skills.

They spent their time off together in Hans' Berlin apartment but Tilly resisted Hans' overtures for them to live together. "I just can't do it right now," was always her response. Only together a few months, Hans was in love.

And then Tilly suddenly had excuses about spending time with Hans. "Work, Hans. It's not you, it's me." Hans knew well that line, he had used it often enough to break up with former girlfriends.

Hans was unprepared for that cold, rainy night Tilly pounded on his door several weeks after she stopped seeing him. "I'm frightened, Hans," he remembered her saying as she took off her rain-soaked jacket and rain hat. "I don't think I was followed,"

As he listened intently to her story, he felt horror at having been involved with her and considered his life might now be in danger. Tilly knew Hans was an ally of German Chancellor Becker.

Tilly disclosed she was a prostitute, sleeping with high level politicians and businessmen and reported directly to the Chancellor on any information she obtained from her clients. Especially on anyone in the political opposition. The Chancellor provided her with money and security, she provided him with information. "But I never, ever disclosed my relationship with you, Hans!"

Tilly planned to graduate from the Humboldt University of Berlin. Her plan was to become a fashion model but she took the position her father's friend, the Chancellor, offered her as an assistant in the Tourism Department.

She found she could manipulate powerful men through her use of flirtations and sexual favors to get anything she wanted. All the more power to her if the men were married and fearful of the relationship being exposed. Tilly used blackmail to get information for the Chancellor.

Herr Worthermann was too smart to become entangled with her sexually but one of his closest allies, Major Harther, was not. It didn't take Tilly long to get the Major, who was married, under her sexual spell. Harther enjoyed his Asbach Uralt brandy and often disclosed workings of the High Command to her after particularly robust drinking and sex.

It was through Major Harther she discovered a secure website detailing plans for the new Third Reich with the neo-Nazi cells in New York City and Paris. In addition to the names of neo-Nazis in the United States she had learned from Harther the workings of the medical facility at Willowist. Nazis embedded in the United States? Working from a diplomatic protected building? Seeking to create a coup? A WWII Nazi being treated and kept alive there? She was frightened that Franz Worthermann would have her murdered because she knew too much about his operations.

Worthermann decided that Major Harther's drinking and his increasingly erratic behavior, coupled with his affair with Tilly, made it time for Harther to resign from the High Command. A Soon after his resignation several soldiers quietly broke into the apartment Tilly and Harther used for their sexual escapades. Tilly had left the apartment earlier to get cigarettes, and as Major Harther lay in bed, his last vision was of a 9 mm with a silencer aimed at his forehead. To explain Harther's disappearance, Worthermann created the story that Major Harther was a traitor to the German military and went AWOL.

One of the soldiers stayed in the apartment awaiting Tilly's return.As Tilly walked back from the neighborhood convenient store she saw a soldier leaving the apartment and knew immediately Harther was dead, and she would be next. Tilly turned and ran as it began to rain and headed toward Hans' place.

"You would be surprised at what men say after sex while lounging in bed," Hans remembered Tilly saying. "I knew business and political deals they never told their wives." Hans tried to recall everything he had confided in her after their lovemaking.

"Things changed", she continued, "when I learned from a client that the Chancellor was terrified of Franz Worthermann, who was now the power behind the scenes. He is running the country, Hans. And he is a Nazi."

Tilly went on. "I had a regular client, Major Harther, a confidant and hitman for Wortherman.He often would tell me about offshore accounts Worthermann set up for German officials. Worthermann blackmails government officials to keep control of them. And doesn't hesitate to murder them or their families if they don't cooperate with him.

One night in particular Major Harther mentioned he was looking into Willowist accounts, that's when he disappeared. I care about you and was terrified our relationship might be discovered and Worthermann come after you.

There is something strange is going on at Willowist. Herr Worthermann and the High Command have got some old Nazi being kept alive in your medical facility. They have saved the lives of many Nazis who have been the target of Nazi hunters but this is different. There is unusual interest in Willowist."

"I have nothing to do with whatever is going on at the Willowist medical research facility, that's kept completely separate from my job as administrator of the main Willowist facility. That's a 99 year lease the United States signed with Germany once WWII ended. This area once had a large German population, and what is now the medical research facility was once a hospital for the German community.

"All I do is make sure these old farts have an upscale retirement," Hans noted.

Tilly took a shot of Jägermeister.

"Worthermann has developed Nazi cells and is planning a coup in Germany to restart the Nazi movement. I think he is deranged, Hans, Worthermann thinks there will be a worldwide uprising of Nazis and a return of the Third Reich!"

"That's unbelievable! How does this all affect me, Tilly?"

"Your life may be in danger. I know from Major Harther there are rumors you have been moving some money yourself into an offshore account. If Worthermann finds out…..", Tilly's voice faded out.

She continued, "This may help protect you. It's the location of a secure website with names, addresses and contacts of Nazi cell members. It is impossible to access though, its got rings of security. But Worthermann can't touch you if he knows you have this information for fear if it becomes public his plans will be ruined. Don't try to access it. Any attempt is logged, and the Nazis will know."

"This information won't protect me! It may have sealed my death warrant, Tilly. If Worthermann knows I have it he will have me killed."

"The Chancellor arranged safe travel for me to Paris, where I can hide out until things calm down, I want you to know that you are the only one I really care about. The others were just 'johns'. Just work. I love you Hans.I have to go."

Tilly walked quickly down the deserted street toward the car that would take her to the private airfield and boarded the jet arranged by the Chancellor.

CHAPTER 13

WILLOWIST

The long dark haired woman in his office smiled as he admired her body and good looks. Remarkable, really, he thought, for a woman in her early fifties to be such a gorgeous, sexually active woman. And how she called him "sexist" for thinking such thoughts he remembered.

Hans pulled her toward him and gave her a long, deep kiss.

"When the time is right we will be having a glass of Schloss Johannisberg Riesling on a deck overlooking the ocean. We have a future together," he lied.

He began to unbutton her blouse as they tumbled onto the couch, kissing fiercely.

Hans loved her wild, sensual embraces and gave into his physical needs even though he knew this affair was going to end badly for her. But soon he wouldn't need her anymore.

Hans was like an affable salesman who could sell anything, sociable and well-liked by the residents. Even though he hated senior citizens, he constantly promoted the benefits of joining the Willowist community, such as the luxury living conditions at Willowist.

To live at Willowist, the senior citizen, age 55 and over was required to turn over all monetary assets like IRA's, bank accounts, social security monies to him to be deposited in a Willowist account. in their individual name but with full authority by him to manage the account.

Monthly fees would be withdrawn electronically from each resident's account to cover all living expenses at Willowist, and the resident would never have to take out their purse or wallet, even for trips to New York City for the Broadway shows.

Hans was slowly and carefully withdrawing a generic "administrative fee" from every resident every month. He planned on having enough money soon to find Tilly Miller and live together comfortably away from the politics and problems of Germany.

Hans did not trust the militant group of the German High Command quietly moving into high ranking government positions. He knew if Chancellor Becker were overthrown, his own life was in danger of a purge of any officials allied with the Chancellor.

His "insurance" in case he was targeted by the neo-Nazis was the information given to him by Tilly. Hans was confident Becker's allies in the American government would protect him but he preferred to disappear with Tilly to some beautiful island.

The long dark haired woman dressed and said goodbye. She never liked having this romantic fling with Hans, she thought him gross, but her superiors in the German High Command wanted her to keep tabs on Hans and his activities at Willowist. She was to kill him when Worthermann gave the order.

She had espoused the neo-Nazi movement when her brother offered to induct her into his Nazi group. His death at the hands of a German policeman during an aborted robbery attempt he was involved in merely ignited the lingering hatred she had for the German government. She was tired of the German people having to apologize for Hitler's actions. She was tired of Chancellor Becker and his American friends. She became a disciple of Herr Worthermann.

When Herr Worthermann tested her loyalty directing her to murder a German police officer, she placed the gun to head of the police officer she had seduced and felt no guilt pulling the trigger. Her intelligence and loyalty was well-received by the High Command, and she became a trusted member of their inner circle.

"Heil Hitler" Lady Vikki whispered to herself as she returned to her apartment. She was a Nazi and proud of it.

CHAPTER 14

WILLOWIST

Sophia and George decided to go with the Swoops to observe a Viagra Night social which were held occasionally as the Willowist staff was concerned too many socials close together would be too exciting for the male residents to handle.Although dubbed as a night social, it was more early evening because the Willowist residents were not late-night partygoers.

"Now George, keep away from those little blue pills or I'll have to run out of here before you attack me" Sophia teased.

"Very funny," George blushed, eye twitched. Although he secretly imagined what a tryst would be like with Sophia.

"I am going to see what's doing," Liz laughed. "Maybe Mary Margret and I will get lucky tonight!" Her infectious laughter spread to Sophia and George.

The ballroom lighting was indirect and subdued, not the raucous atmosphere of the polka party nights. A long buffet table with jumbo shrimp, oysters, and other snacks was in the center of the room. Cafe tables were set up throughout the room with colorful floral arrangements on each table. And of course the little blue Viagra pills in large bowls with a scooper were strategically placed on tables. There were two registered nurses from the assisted living wing on duty in case the residents became overly excited and needed medical attention.

"No live band tonight," Mary Margret remarked. "There will be a lot of oldies played by the DJ to set the mood. Lots of slow dancing."

"That's the only kind of dancing the men here can do," Liz howled, causing nearby ladies to join in the laughter.

Elvis Presley's "Can't Help Falling In Love" wafted through the room. "Remember, we are just pretending to be a couple," Sophia whispered to George, causing him to blush and eye to twitch as she they walked to the dance floor.

Eleanor Colbert pushed her way through a few ladies to get Dr. Sam's attention. "Hello, Doctor! You don't usually attend these parties, how are you?" Dr. Sam's hearing aid buzzed loud enough for her to hear it. "How about coming to my room," he bellowed, not realizing his voice carried. Some of the female residents giggled at his outburst.

"Oh, Doctor! Yes! I would love to see your apartment," Eleanor answered. She thought even if nothing happens sexually she could get him away from the other "vultures" as she referred to the other women at the Viagra party.

Lizzie focused her attention on 66 year old Jack O'Corra, while Mary Margret chose to stay with Sophia and George. O'Corra was a professional boxer, according to him. His family laughed whenever asked about his boxing career. "He danced around, never took a punch, the big coward. He'd fall down if the other boxer got close."

Lizzie knew what to expect when she talked to O'Corra. Every conversation with him included his lament that "Lawrence Welk stole the Hurdy Gurdy Waltz that I wrote." Lizzie knew of course that was a fantasy O'Corra held onto. Still, he was a male willing to dance with her and that was good enough for her.

Sophia noticed a glance and eye contact between Lady Vikki and Hans, the administrator, which confirmed to her the rumors Lady Vikki and Hans were lovers.

Surprisingly, the music was not all slow. The "Bobbys", as Sophia referred to them, got some play time. Bobby Darren. Bobby Rydell. Bobby Vinton. Bobby Vee. "Bobby Bobby", she smiled, remembering her younger days.

The Stroll came on and George, Sophia and the Swoops joined the stroll line. "Cat would have enjoyed this tonight as I just explained to her what the Stroll is. How dancers form two lines facing one another and take half steps in same direction, at the end of the line one dancer on each side turns into the middle and they 'stroll' to the end of the line where they rejoin the line."

Sophia momentarily flinched when she turned into the line and saw Viola across from her as her stroll partner! Although Sophia offered a smile, Viola just stared straight ahead and did not acknowledge Sophia.

Cat, who was not there, was the only one Sophia confided in about her past relationship with Viola. Even George didn't notice the tension between Sophia and Viola, although the Crew was well aware of it.

By 8:30 pm the party was over and most of the women went to their apartments alone. For the others, it was random as to which couples the Viagra actually helped. Eleanor Cobert put on the 10 O'Clock news alone in her apartment. As soon as they entered his apartment, Dr. Sam put on the television, sat on the couch with her and fell asleep. "At least I started something with him," Eleanor Colbert mused, "he is now my man."

CHAPTER 15

Intelligence had come in to the Bri team that the German High Command was planning a major event with some former Nazi concentration camp leaders. The Bri had clashed with neo-Nazi groups in France and had eliminated a cell of over twenty neo-Nazis. The Nazis had a meeting in a farmhouse in Lyon, and they never knew what hit them. Fetterman and his team trapped the Nazis in the farmhouse then set it afire, and the arson was never discovered by the French inspectors and police.

"Still sketchy information but this one looks to be a big one. He is going to Philadelphia with a few of his top officers to attend the Super Bowl. He isn't a football fan." Fetterman explained to his team. "Whatever Worthermann is planning looks to be that day and a unifying event for the Nazi cells."

JoJo, anything you can add?"

"Getting there, Chief. Internet chatter picking up," Josephine Gantz answered. "There is talk of a coup."JoJo Gantz was a tough, frontline fighter during some of the unpublicized skirmishes with Iran military. Muscular and stocky, she never hesitated to be the first one to engage the enemy.

"Our intelligence was on the mark. Agreed its something soon. Worthermann definitely involved so its big," Jo-Jo added. "If he is planning a coup of the German government but why would he be in the United States?" JoJo's intelligence team had discovered Worthermann was planning a trip to the United States in the near future to coincide with Worthermann's increasing references to " the New Day", that is the return of the Third Reich and the new world order.

Fetterman and his team had no use for the legal process. They would take no chances a jury would sympathize with any elderly former Nazi leader. In their nineties with failing health, the Nazi's were rarely deported or even jailed. The Bri executed every man or woman Nazi they found, usually with the complicity of the authorities.

Fetterman remembered a raid in England. An old woman living alone and quietly outside of Broadchurch had been a brutal, murderous officer in the Nazi regime who had accounted for hundreds of deaths of Jews.She personally set people afire, tortured and killed men, women and children.Hitler gave her numerous medals.She escaped to England after the allies invaded France and with the help of false ID's settled into a quiet life in Broadchurch. Fetterman credited JoJo's intelligence network in finding her. When JoJo smashed open the door of her country cabin, the former Nazi sat up in bed and knew her nightmares of being discovered were happening.JoJo put the 3 shots in the woman's head. 3 shots close together just above her eyes. The calling card of the Bri.

"JoJo, lets shake things up a little. We need a high profile hit, get Worthermann to come out of hiding," Fetterman said.

CHAPTER 16

BERLIN

Brogan Fields entered the private office of Chancellor Becker.

"Sir, there are several protests planned in opposition to your ties to the American President." Fields omitted saying "I should know, Herr Worthermann and I organized them."

"Damn them, Brogan. I have built my career on advocating for a global economy, global considerations," Becker replied.

"Yes. But there is a growing nationalism and distrust of other countries."

"I am not giving into a few loud hate mongers."

"Sir, there are members of the Bundestag who oppose your global views. And your ties with the Americans."

Chancellor Becker was a moderate who promised policies that would jump start a sagging German economy. A former German Ambassador to the United Nations, he developed friendships with leaders of other countries and especially with the American ambassador who introduced him to the American President.

Becker met privately with the American President once, and the two had a special hotline set up with direct ties to one another. The private meeting was in a conference room at the United Nations and arranged without fanfare or attention.

Both were advocates of a global economy, and both shared concerns about the increasing rebirth of Nazism. The American President was "not the brightest bulb" Becker often confided in his Cabinet but "he is a good ally and understands the danger Franz Worthermann brings to the international community with his Nazi beliefs and growing popular support." Privately, Becker had concerns the President didn't fully understand that there were Nazi cells operating in several American cities and werer capable of terrorist acts.

Becker's affable nature and ability to compromise earned him the respect of world leaders. His Administration delivered as promised and during his first year there was success in lowering unemployment and encouraging business development.

Brogan Fields was a neo-Nazi and a longtime friend of both Chancellor Becker and Franz Worthermann. Becker hired Fields as his personal assistant, not knowing Fields reported Becker's every move to Worthermann.

An early scandal, not the Chancellor's fault, with several of his cabinet members caught soliciting prostitutes dampened some of the enthusiasm of his leadership.

SOMEWHERE IN GERMANY

Martin King was the lead story just a year and a half into Becker's term. Sex and corruption. King was in charge of government security. Unknown to Chancellor Becker, King was taking huge kickbacks from companies providing weapons and other equipment to law enforcement. King also was running a prostitution ring, enticing local officials to have sex with prostitutes while secretly filming them. Blackmail gave King the power to control the actions of government officials. All this added to his political power and increasing fortune.

One of his prostitutes, Tilly Miller, slept with high level Nazis tied into Chancellor Becker's enemy, Fran Worthermann. Tilly knew how to play the game and was a good source for the Chancellor to learn information about the workings of the High Command. But Tilly's cover was blown, and King knew her days were numbered. At Chancellor Becker's behest, King arranged for a jet to take her to a safe house in Paris.

King, through a shell corporation, purchased an chalet with upscale amenities in the mountains. Used exclusively for his prostitution and blackmailing activities, he invited one of Chancellor Becker's political allies, Senator Leon Mueller to visit. King was aware of Mueller's predilection towards young women. And recently the Senator had begun turning the tables on King, threatening to have him arrested if he didn't include the Senator on the moneymaking schemes.

King sent one of his prized prostitutes, Sherrianne Sisco, for a tryst with the Senator. Sisco commanded

$6000 in American dollars for a twenty four hour session but was becoming too independent of King. Sisco decided she was known in the right circles and no longer needed to answer to King or pay him his commission. He decided to take care of the two problems at once.

The chalet had a maid who cooked and cleaned but always left before any arrivals and never saw or knew who King's visitors were. King arranged for the wine delivered to the chalet to contain a powerful sedative. Senator Mueller and Sherrianne Sisco took a steamy shower together and kissed deeply and hard. He threw her on the bed, caressed her, then had wild sexual intercourse, ending with them both collapsing into a deep sleep. When Senator Mueller awoke, he rolled over in the bed and put his arms around Sisco. Sleepily, he felt a wetness on his arm, and when he opened his eyes he saw her throat had been sliced, killing her, the knife lying next to him.

Pictures were taken by one of King's operatives showing the Senator's earlier sexual escapades with Sisco, the dead girl and the bloody knife. From that moment on, Senator Leon Mueller was a staunch supporter of King and King's boss, Chancellor Becker.

King's mistake was to try to control the news media by blackmailing the news director of a national news organization.Instead of giving in to King's demands, the news director made public the sexual escapades of Senator Mueller and his ties to Martin King which he had been anonymously sent. The story ran on the German national news and included footage obtained from King's enemies of King trafficking in young women. The public outrage over the scandal threatened to spill over to Chancellor Becker.

"Brogan, we need to come out strong on this and disavow any knowledge of King's activities. I will give a forceful statement denouncing him. Make a list of reporters who have been friendly to me, and we'll give them an exclusive interview with me."

"Will take care of that right away," Fields said. And thought to himself, "just as soon after I alert Franz what you are doing."

Once Brogan Fields spoke with him, Franz Worthermann quickly called a news conference saying to "drain the swamp" in Berlin, using terminology a former United States President had used. Worthermann used the King scandal to bolster his own image as a reformer before Chancellor Becker could publicly react to the King scandal.

Chancellor Becker made sure King was prosecuted, and the Chancellor's Administration survived the incident. But Chancellor Becker's reputation took a hit while Franz Worthermann's gained credibility. Becker began to think his former childhood friend was going to run against him. But Worthermann had much bigger plans.

"Keep me informed what Becker is doing politically, Brogan. The people of Germany should not be saddled with an idiot who bows down to the Americans, and lets all of Europe control him. Keep up the opposition to him in Parliament, keep him occupied while I get prepare the rise of the Third Reich.

On my signal I want you to assassinate him. Everything will happen at the same time. His cabinet members will be murdered, and there will be what will be reported as a terrorist attack on the old people at Willowist when the entire community there will be destroyed. That will distract attention from our real goal of getting rid of the German medical research facility. I don't want the Americans sniffing around in there trying to tie anything to me personally."

"Do you want me to arrange for safe transportation of our German workers there, Franz?"

"They will be safely removed."

CHAPTER 17

The Willowist bus trips to New York City were a hoot, as George described them. Listening over the bus speakers to taped Abbot and Costello shows, singing songs like Side By Side and Mitch Miller sing along songs. Even the Crew dropped their nastiness on the bus trips.

Surprisingly the casino near Times Square continued to offer vouchers for gambling, drinks and food, even though some of the seniors took the free buffets and other free gifts and turned the vouchers in for cash without doing any gambling. It was a free trip to New York City with free food and drinks. "The casinos can afford it," Esther Chaney sniffed, as she enjoyed a free bourbon and water.

Suzy Petuch loved the slots while Rosy DeStefano played blackjack in the High Stakes room. Dinner was served in the private casino dining room for those residents at the casino. Many residents headed out into downtown Manhattan to explore the sights and sounds of the City.

This particular Saturday the Crew had tickets for the matinee of the hit show Wicked while some residents strolled Fifth Avenue. Ellen's Stardust Diner where the waiters and waitress occasionally stand on the tables and sing show tunes was a big attraction to the Willowist residents. And the "food is good", as they frequently pointed out to other Willowist residents.

As usual on the bus Sophia and George would take a taxi together while Cat would find her way on her own to La Vigna, an small Italian restaurant tucked away from the tourist areas. They joined the bus trips to keep up appearances but met in private to discuss strategy. By the time the bus returned to Willowist, the residents were too tired and sleepy to be concerned about the activities of the three undercover operatives.

CHAPTER 18

CALI, COLOMBIA

El Gringo reach for his satellite phone over one of the girls asleep next to him in bed. Billy Green's exited voice magnified his headache from a night of partying, drinking and sex. "Take it down a notch, Dumbass," the druglord yelled into the phone. "And you two whores get out here,"he screamed at the girls in bed with him. "Tell my bodyguards to pay you and then get lost."

"Boss, we have a break in the Olivanti case. One of my guys confirmed Olivanti is in the states and we should have his new name and location soon."

"Idiot! Don't call to tell me you don't have Olivanti yet. I want to know when you find him. When you do, remember that he is not to be touched. I am going to exact Colombian revenge on him personally when you get him."

El Gringo slammed the phone down. "Where's my morning aguardiante?" he screamed at his bodyguard.

CHAPTER 19

The menu at La Vigna was given orally by the waiter, who spoke Italian to customers who were fluent, such as Sophia, George and Cat. The waiter was tall, bald and looked to be in his 50's. They referred to him as "Father Waiter" because in his black outfit Cat laughed that he looked like a priest.

La Vigna had no main dining room, there was a center bar area surrounded by doors to individual private rooms. Privacy and discretion were valued by customers and staff. Several times federal agents tried to subpoena the restaurant's reservation book but were never able to convince a federal judge there was a legitimate purpose to investigate it. The rumors of it being a meeting place of high level organized crime figures was never proven.

"George, any latest intel from the internet,?"

"Lots of chatter, Sophia. Worthermann's men have been on a rampage, killing local politicians and police loyal to Becker. Worthermann apparently has a spy in Becker's inner circle but I haven't been able to him."

"A spy?"

"Yes, Cat. Someone close to Becker is reporting back to Worthermann.

Worthermann is becoming more and more popular, and his pro-Nazi beliefs have a huge following. However, in the public opinion polls the German public views Becker as a likeable leader. It gets a little sticky for Becker when people are asked if they support his particular policies."

"How about the medical building, George, when can Cat and I try to get a look inside? Those old abandoned bomb shelter tunnels that lead from the woods into the basement of the medical building will be good access,"Sophia observed.

"Not yet. Too dangerous. Until I get a way into the system, any failed attempts will alert the Germans."

CHAPTER 20

Using the internet and the local library Chrissy Rice was able to compile a list of several individuals who knew Franz Worthermann in some capacity. The first five she contacted slammed the phone down without commenting. Number six, however, was willing to meet Rice in a public place, a hip coffee shop with cozy couches and excellent espresso.

"Thank you for meeting with me," Chrissy shook Number Six's hand. Chrissy promised not to use names, and this thirty-something pretty German woman wanted privacy.

"What's this all about, I haven't heard from Franz in months, is he in trouble?"

"Not at all! I am doing a college research paper, and he is one of the top German leaders," she replied easily, trying to put Number Six at ease. "People really admire him."

"How did my name come up?"

"I saw your picture in a news article with him and through facial recognition found your information. Tell me anything you want to about him."

Number Six sipped on her espresso, eyeing Chrissy carefully.

"Not much I can add. I attended a lecture he spoke at, was impressed and did some volunteer work with him at a Church. All I can tell you he is intelligent and committed to improving the lives of Germans. Why? What's your interest in Franz Worthermann?"

"Did he mention the neo-Nazi movement?," Chrissy said quietly.

"So thats your game? Going to mock the Nazi movement in Germany?"

"Not at all," Chriss replied, slightly shaken at Number Six's aggressive attitude.

"No. He didn't mention the Nazi movement. He was speaking at a religious conference. Look, sorry to waste your time but I don't have anything else to add." Number Six abruptly walked away.

The German reading a newspaper at the cafe table nearby watched as Chrissy left. With his cell phone he texted a picture of Chrissy Rice to Franz Worthermann. The accompanying message said "our friend met the American." It was Worthermann who had Number Six agree to meet with Chrissy Rice to find out why Rice was so interested in him.

As Number Six entered her apartment she fell limp as the large hands of the intruder crushed her throat. Worthermann didn't like his men to leave any loose ends, and Angel was good at tying up loose ends.

CHAPTER 21

WILLOWIST

Sophia and Bingo Bob continued their friendly talks at the gym, on the porch and walking through the gardens.

"Sophia, can I ask a very personal question?"

"You can ask, not sure if I will answer."

"Are you and George a couple?"

Sophia tensed. She was concerned about keeping personal relationships separate from missions. But it didn't take long for her to realize she was beginning to care, really care, for Bob. It was important to the mission to give the appearance she and George were a couple, which explains to the other residents why they are constantly together.

While the thoughts were going through her mind, Bob put his arm around her and gave her a firm, deep kiss. She kissed back, then pulled away.

"Bob, we can't. Lets just keep this as friends."

"I think about you all the time, Sophia, I just want to be with you."

"Just give me time to sort some things out. I don't want to lead you on, and I don't want to hurt George".

"I've seen you with George, it doesn't seem there is really anything going on between you two."

"I have to get back to my apartment, Cat and I are going to a movie," Sophia lied.

The next morning at 6 am Sophia and Bob did a run together around the gym track, both doing their best to avoid the awkwardness of the kiss in the garden.

"You and George going to breakfast?"

"Not until 8:30, George is doing some reading and I want to relax in the steam room. You can join us for breakfast if you want.

"See you there!"

There was no one in the gym nor in the huge women's locker room with its private sauna and steam room. Sophia turned on the steam room heat, wrapped a towel around her hair and her waist and sat down for a relaxing steam.

After a few minutes Sophia felt the sting of the steam and realized the setting was too hot. As she pushed against the steam room door, it didn't respond. She pushed several times and wondered why the door wasn't opening. She screamed for help and felt herself getting dizzy. Sophia felt her skin was on fire as she stumbled around in the steam room and fell over.

CHAPTER 22

PARIS

The second floor apartment Chancellor Becker had arranged for Tilly Miller was larger and more luxurious than she had expected. And while enjoying a lovely view of the Seine she poured a glass of sweet white Zinfandel and considered her situation.

Chancellor Becker assured her she would be safe and to keep a low profile at the Paris apartment where the bodyguard outside the apartment would protect her until things calmed down. "You will be an important witness when we can arrest Worthermann and his Nazis. Martin King and I will make sure you are protected."

What Chancellor Becker didn't realize was that Brogan Fields had access to the Chancellor's laptop. When Becker was at a cabinet meeting, Fields searched the files until he found it. "TM. Rue de Seine. 341. 236." It didn't take long for Fields to decipher that note. "Tilly Miller. 341 Rue de Seine. Apartment 236." He passed that information on to Worthermann.

Tilly regretted ever getting mixed up with the Nazis. Sleeping with the politicians and businessmen and using their indiscretions to help Becker keep power didn't concern her. "Hell, I planned on Chancellor Becker to get me into the fashion mags sooner or later." She didn't anticipate Becker planned on using her to get to Worthermann, who scared the hell out of her.

Another wine. "Damn Becker! A witness against Nazis! I could understand some jealous wife coming after me for screwing her husband and me ending up a witness in divorce court. But Nazis? Who the hell thinks there are still Nazis around?

Maybe if I make a deal with Worthermann to give him all my computer files on his wayward men he will let me alone,"she considered. That's it. I will find a way to offer him information for my freedom. Then they can all go to hell, and I will stop whoring and get into the fashion business."

More wine. Tilly looked in the mirror and felt she was still young enough, attractive enough to be a model. She felt a sense of sadness come over her. She felt used. And lied to. Tilly fell asleep sobbing.

She was awakened by a loud banging on the door. "Who is it?"

"Package delivery."

Tilly was alarmed to see a very large man holding a package. She had a gun for protection but it was not close by the door.

"I didn't order anything, you must have the wrong apartment."

"M'am, please. Just sign for this package."

Tilly opened the door carefully and accepted the package. When she opened it, she screamed and vomited. It was the head of Sebastian Herron, a former soccer player and lover. She had met Sebastian at a soccer game, introduced by mutual friends. They spent several days and nights together enjoying a wild, sexual relationship that turned into mutual feelings of love. He broke off their relationship, and it wasn't until months later he hadn't wanted her to know he began to have symptoms of multiple sclerosis. He was one of the few men she had feelings for.

NEW YORK CITY

The drug house in the Village reeked of stale cigarettes, cheap scotch and weed. Billy Green put a gun to the head of the middle aged hippie lying on the couch.

"Yo, man! Who you with? I am cool."

"Relax, asshole. This isn't a bust. I just want to know the name of the DEA agent you are working with."

The hippie awkwardly tried to grab Green's gun but Green smashed him with his free hand, breaking the hippie's nose. "Who put you undercover asshole?"

This was the first real lead Billy Green had to a DEA agent who might have information on the whereabouts of Angelo Olivanti.

"I have a deal! I have a deal! Get the hell out of here," the hippie screamed.

Green used his silencer and shot the hippie in the leg. "Who?"

The hippie blurted out "Thigood." Green fired a shot through the hippie's heart.

Roger Thigood. Green knew him well. They had actually done some drug busts together. Straight by the book agent. Won't be able to buy information on Olivanti from this guy. He actually thinks he can change the world, Green considered as he called El Gringo.

"Good and bad news, Boss. I have the name of someone who might have the Olivanti witness protection info. But the bad news he won't talk."

"Bring him to me,' El Gringo demanded.

Roger Thigood was driving on a Pennsylvania country road to his gun club for some target practice. Two black Ford Tahoe's had been behind him several miles, and he considered his options. He punched in his office numbers on his cell but before the phone connected one of the Tahoe's was alongside him and several guns were pointed on him. He tried to take evasive action but the Tahoe rammed the side of his car, and he skidded off the road, through some high grass and came to a stop in a cornfield. Thigood passed out when he hit his head on the steering wheel.

When he awoke he felt ice cold liquid in the vein of his right arm. Slightly groggy he realized he was on a cot with an IV in his arm.

"We can do this the easy way or the hard way," he heard a vaguely familiar voice. His eyes focused on fellow DEA agent Billy Green.

"Bill Green? What the fuck? Where am I?," his head started to throb.

"Never mind that Rogie, we just need some information and then you will be home before you know it," Billy Green lied.

Thigood struggled to stay awake. "I don't understand."

Billy Green lowered his voice, "Rogie, I don't want to see you get hurt. Just tell me how to locate Angelo

Olivanti, you were in charge of getting him in the witness protection program. You were in a car accident and flown here to Colombia just to answer a few questions. I promise you, if you cooperate all will be ok. Otherwise, please listen Rogie, these guys will make you talk one way or the other, and it won't be pleasant. "You, Billy? Playing with the cartels?"

Billy Green handed Thigood over to two tall, thin men with tattoos covering every inch of their visible skin. "Please, Rogie. Tell them what they want to know. I don't want to see you hurt."

Thigood was blindfolded and tied to a chair. His body shook when the ice water raced down his head and onto his body.

"I am going to make it easy on you, just tell me where is Angelo Olivanti? What's his new identity and where is he?" El Gringo barked.

"I don't know." Thigood felt a powerful blow to the back of his head.

"Once more, where is Olivanti?"

Thigood was dazed and tried to understand what was going on.

"I don't know who you are talking about."

He screamed in pain as he felt wet, sticky blood drip from where the knife sliced his cheek.

Thigood drifted in and out of consciousness for several hours. Exhausted and in throbbing pain, Thigood finally said "Cusatis" and passed out.

"Who's Cusatis?", El Gringo challenged Billy Green.

"A special agent. I know him. I should be able to get Olivanti's witness protection information from him without bringing him here. He can be bought one way or another. He is a family man with kids he loves, included a paralyzed daughter who needs expensive medical treatment, not all of it covered by insurance."

"Do it!" El Gringo shouted as he shot and killed Agent Thigood. "Or you're next."

CHAPTER 23

WILLOWIST

Sophia awoke on the floor of the locker room. She had been laid down on some towels, a towel wrapped up like a pillow, a towel still wrapped around her body, still wet from the steam room. She got up slowly and looked around the steam room, the steam had been turned off, and nothing seemed out of place. The broom handle which had been apparently used to prevent her from opening the steam room from the inside was lying near the door.

She sat on a bench a few minutes and tried to figure out what was going on. She and Bingo Bob had run together, she went into the locker room and decided to take a steam bath. The door was blocked, she had difficulty breathing and passed out.

"Who locked me in? Who took me out, probably saving my life?" She wondered if her undercover assignment was discovered. Or if someone mistook her for someone else they wanted to hurt?

Sophia showered and dressed. It was still the breakfast hour, and she needed to talk to George and Cat.

She gave them the signal she had to talk, and they went separately to one of the garden areas where they agreed to meet. After she explained what happened, George went to his room to access the security cameras for the gym.

"There are no cameras inside the locker room but at 7:12 am someone entered, left at 7:15 am. At 7:20 am someone entered and left at 7:26 am. Its difficult to make out any clear features but both looked like women. I will use my software recognition to see if I can identify your assailant.

Cat wondered "why would someone try to harm you, then change their mind and save you?"

"Did anything unusual happen to you or George? Do you think my cover has been exposed."

"All quiet," Cat replied. "We haven't done anything yet to arouse suspicions."

"Come over here, Sophia, one of these images is confirmed on my computer."

"Viola Lepere!" Sophia recognized her immediately.

Viola Lepere finished breakfast with the Swope Sisters and joined the Crew in one of the tv lounges. Everyday they would watch reruns of the old Dallas soap opera together. They routinely good naturedly argued over which one of them was what character. They all wanted to be seen as Miss Ellie but only Rosy was unanimously called J.R.

The Crew look astonished when Sophia came in somewhat aggressively and approached Viola. Suzy Petuch whispered "This was bound to blow up". "Shut up," Rosy told her.

"We have to talk. Now!" Sophia was face-to-face with Viola. "Outside."

No one interfered as Sophia and Viola went onto the porch.

"You damn bitch, I could have died in that steam room."

Sophia turned away from Viola as she heard George running towards them yelling "Stop Sophia! Stop! She was the second one on the camera, she is the one that saved you!"

Through tears, Viola, shaking, didn't say a word.

Confused, Sophia looked back and forth to George and Viola.

"It's true Sophia. I have been following you, wondering why you are here. I have watched you in the gym with Bingo Bob, walk in the gardens, talk to Cat. This morning I left when you went into the locker room but saw Alma go in, she never goes to the gym. I know she has been jealous of you and George. When she left so quickly I went back in, saw you were locked in the steam room, got you out and put you on some towels."

Sophia was stunned. "Alma? Tried to kill me? Out of jealousy for George? You saved me?"

"Alma has mental issues, probably was off her meds. She will be taken back to the mental hospital."

Sophia was uncharacteristically shaken. "Viola, how can I thank you? How could I have blamed you? I am so sorry. So sorry!"

"Seeing you again, Sophia, brought back all those awful high school memories when Scott died in your car. I have come to realize the accident was not your fault."

The Crew eavesdropping by the window retreated to the tv, and George awkwardly walked away.

"Lets talk, Viola. I have missed you!"

Sophia and Viola avoided the Gossip Room and ordered tea as they sat in deep, luxurious Hemingway leather chairs in an alcove. Both were visibly emotional as they spoke.

"When I saw you were trapped in the steam room and might die, I realized how awful this antagonism I have felt for you is," Viola said through tears. "We had so many wonderful times growing up."

"I know, Viola. For years I lived and relived what happened that night with Scott. I never cheated with him, you know. No one was more important to me than you."

Viola took a sip of tea."Where to start, Sophia? Family? Married? Kids?"

"My life has been boring, Viola. After my brother was killed in Vietnam and my parents died, I went into government service. Dated occasionally but never met Mr. Right", Sophia lied. "Saved my money to retire and here I am. What about you?"

Sophia wanted to divert attention from herself and why she was at Willowist.

"Isn't it strange how we can sum up our entire lives in a couple of sentences.After college I worked in the healthcare industry, got married and divorced, no kids. Sold some stock I had acquired and here I am."

"And you are the leader of the Crew!," Sophia laughed.

"And you, a retired bureaucrat? I don't know, Sophia. That just doesn't seem like the patriotic, intense girl I knew and loved. There has to be more to your story!"

"I wish there were," Sophia replied. "Hey, remember the time in sixth grade we dressed up like Daisy Duck and Minnie Mouse for the class Halloween party? And you started crying when Johnny Longo pulled your mouse ears off," Sophia laughed.

"Haha. And the time we were in charge of stage production that year and Mrs. Drasher was bent over with her butt to the audience making a change on the set and we accidentally opened the curtain, causing all the kids to hoot and holler!"

Both women were laughing, crying and hugging each other. The Gossip Room crowd at Willowist turned their attention to other residents because Sophia and Viola were no longer interesting since the reconcilation.

"I don't like it," Rosemary said as the Crew, minus Viola, had drinks in the Gossip Room. "There just is something about Sophia that doesn't fit. She doesn't look and act like a former government employee. And where did she get the money to come here?"

"Give it a rest, Rosy, who cares," Ida responded.

"Yes, Rosy, if Viola reconciled with Sophia, then so be it. Move on, girl", Esther chimed in.

"I haven't found anything unusual about Sophia but she is hiding something," Rosy insisted.

"Oh Rosy, you have to stop watching those old Matlock television shows," Ida laughed.

The Crew focused attention on 80 year old Lilly Matto flirting with 89 year old retired Judge Jack Hewitt. At Willowist, a former judge, doctor, lawyer or other professional was a solid status catch for a Willowist woman.

NEW YORK CITY

It was on one of the bus trips to the city that Lady Vikki slipped away from the others. Making sure she wasn't followed, she went to an upscale coffee shop on the Upper West Side. Her contact person was already seated. The conversation was in German.

"You weren't followed?"

"No. I'll pick up something at Gucci's or somewhere and if anyone asks, I was shopping."

"It's almost time. Herr Wortherman will have everything you need sent to you and will personally tell you when to do it, are you sure you can do this."

"I would like to do it now. Of course I can do it. These old people are disgusting. Always complaining about something. Self centered."

Lady Vikki and the contact discussed how to carry out Vikki's mission.

"The explosives will be buried around all the buildings at Willowist, including at our German research center. We don't want anything found there connecting the activity to the Nazi movement. When Worthermann gives the order all you will have to do is push the button on the remote you will be given. At a distance of course from all the buildings as they will explode and disintegrate.

"Good riddance to all those old people!"

"There will be a private jet for your return to Germany. Worthermann wants you in his cabinet when the Third Reich is reborn," the contact lied.

Vikki couldn't wait until Worthermann's plan succeeded. The Nazi rule had been lucrative to her family business, and she was one hundred per cent behind the return of the Third Reich. Her father had several businesses, the most successful was manufacturing ammunition. One time the Fuhrer paid a surprise visit to the plant, and personally thanked her father for his help. Lady Vikki's dad became a local celebrity after that visit. She despised Chancellor Becker and his "playing to the international community of idiots" as she described it.

The contact got up to leave first, "Heil Hitler!"

"Heil Hitler!" Vikki replied.

Out of earshot of Lady Vikki, the contact told Worthermann, "She will detonate the explosives that will destroy all of Willowist and our building there. She despises the residents there.

"Just make sure you get rid of her too once we make our move", he replied. "She knows too much and is just a spoiled bitch and socialite who likes to be it news, not really committed to the Nazi rebirth."

"Don't worry. She bought the story about a private jet and that you want her in the cabinet. She is a phony, I agree. Heil Hitler."

"Heil Hitler."

CHAPTER 25

WILLOWIST

George reviewed his plan to hack into the Germans' security system. "I have bypassed two security sites, one more and I will be in their system. But we need to understand, if this attempt fails our mission is over. They will be able to track back to us, and our lives will be in danger. Should I proceed?"

Sophia assured him she was recovered from the steam room attack and ready to work.

"Once I hack into the system I can set up a fake video that will look like nothing go on while you and Cat are extracting the target."

"How would that work, George?"

"For several minutes the German security live video feed will be taken over by me. Anyone looking at the feed will just see a fake video of the site. In other words, you can enter and won't be on camera. But after a few minutes the German system will reset and to back to their live feed, so you have to get in and get out before that happens."

"This is a highly unusual expensive mission for us,

don't you think," Sophia asked. "I never have questioned orders and I am not now, I just don't understand why one more 90 year old something Nazi is worth the time and effort. Why doesn't the US Government just go in and make the extraction?"

George nodded but added there were international implications."The medical research building has diplomatic immunity along with its 99 year lease, and our government is well aware we will be violating international law when we break into it. Chancellor Becker wants the former Nazi leader receiving medical treatment there turned over to him, quietly and without news media attention."

"The Chancellor needs to make Worthermann disappear," Cat offered.

George's screen showed a large green thumbs up icon.

"It's as ready as it's going to get for me to try to hack in. If it works, we will see their security cameras. If it doesn't work, our mission is compromised because the Germans will see the security breach. Our lives could be in danger. Should we proceed?"

Both Sophia and Cat expressed their agreement.

George hit the keyboards and entered the code he had developed. At first the screen flickered, went blank. Then suddenly the three team members were looking into the German medical research entrance way.

"Ok we're in and looking at live shots within the building!"

The first camera showed several German staff members sitting in cubicles working on their computers. Nothing unusual about the kitchen or living quarters. They could see the guard at the elevator sitting behind a desk, apparently on a computer.

The second floor showed what looked like a hospital floor but with more open spaces. There was a nurses' station, and a doctor viewing a computer screen.

The camera in the patient's room focused clearly on the patient, who looked to be comatose and fed through IV's.

"Who is he, George," Sophia wondered. "Any name we would recognize from history?"

George used his facial recognition program and waited for program to process.

"How do we get this old Nazi out alive?" Cat turned to George.

"Not necessarily alive, Cat," Sophia responded. "The Chancellor just wants the body and will make it disappear. No fanfare, nobody to know anything. Then his plan, from what I know, is to arrest Worthermann and disband the High Command. Chancellor Becker supposedly has confidential information on Worthermann that will discredit him and his Nazi movement."

"Who is this old guy," Cat asked.

The facial recognition put a name on the screen.

"Not possible! There must be some mistake," Sophia commented.

Sophia, George and Cat were silent as they stared in disbelief at the name of the patient: Adolph Hitler.

CHAPTER 26

"That's game, son," Barry Selingo motioned to his ten year old son. "You are much improved at eight ball. I taught you how to play pool, now I can't beat you!", he laughed.

The Selingo mansion's rec room would rival an arcade. A home theater, pool table, old PacMan and Donkey Kong video machines, an indoor Olympic swimming pool and skeeball and other traditional arcade games. Barry Jr. never had to leave the house and that's exactly how his dad wanted it. Even though there was a Maserati MC 20 and a Bugatti Divo in the driveway, Barry Selingo drove to work in his five year old Toyota. The less people knew about his personal life and family, the better, he believed.

Selingo's Catering was the trendy operation whose customers included the Philadelphia sports teams venues, colleges throughout Southeastern Pennsylvania and just about every wedding in the wealthy Main Line of Philadelphia. His recent new lucrative contract at the Eagles stadium led to a celebration Barry and his wife Cindy had at their home. For a gathering of family friends, the more traditional menu included Maine lobster, Maryland crabs, steaks, prime ribs, Barry's homemade gourmet burgers and an array of comfort food side dishes, such as baked macaroni, mashed potatoes and garden fresh spinach salads. The big hit of the day for Barry Jr and his friends was the Willy Wonka Chocolate Fountain.

"Life is good," Barry whispered to no one in particular. He, Cindy and Barry Jr. had access to major sporting events, and every major candidate for political office sought campaign donations, returning the favors with even more catering contacts.

This year with the Super Bowl in Philadelphia was especially exciting for Selingo's Catering because the worldwide audience would see commercials touting Selingo's, and their plans to expand into the international sports venues.

Barry wasn't sure who made the recommendation but he was elated to receive a call from someone at the German High Command who was looking for a caterer for some German soccer games. "My first international order," he told Cindy. "Do you know how many people attend soccer games!" Barry took a sip of his Coors beer, flown in a refrigerated compartment directly from the Colorado Coors brewery, courtesy of a German contact named Franz Worthermann. "I like this Worthermann dude," Barry Selingo smiled. "He knows how to foster good relationships with his vendors."

CHAPTER 27

HAMBURG

"It's all set,"Amsel confirmed to Franz Worthermann. "We hired the caterer that will be doing the Super Bowl."

"I want to know everything about this Selingo guy, where he lives, who his family and friends are, what he eats for breakfast. Especially his work routine at the football games, his employees and their families, his truck drivers, security passes. He is our ticket into the stadium and especially the suites on the executive level. Tell him his new German friends want to hire him to cater a suite for the Super Bowl, and money is no problem."

Worthermann looked over his list of allies in the states. He would have mercenaries hired who cared little about why they were hired. Political agendas meant nothing to them. They followed orders, were paid when the job was completed and then go away.

The plan was to use the Selingo warehouse to store the weapons for the German assault, and in the early morning hours of Super Bowl Sunday the soldiers and weapons would go onto the Selingo trucks and enter the stadium with the security passes Selingo was given by the Eagles organization.

Adolf Hitler would be on one of the trucks and taken to the suite with some Worthermann soldiers dressed like nurses and a doctor. No one would give them a second look. The weapons would be placed on room service type carts and taken to the suite reserved for the Germans. Soldiers would take over the media center, and everything would be in place for the announcement that Adolf Hitler is alive.

"I'm on it, Boss."

"Giving Selingo that fake catering contract for soccer won him over for us, sending him a special Coors beer really flattered his ego. He'll do anything for us. Once we use him, kill him."

CHAPTER 28

WILLOWIST

The Gossip Room at Willowist was like a roomful of kindergarten kids all talking at once. Sophia's brush with death, Viola saving Sophia and their reconciliation, Bingo Bob's obvious infatuation with Sophia, Alma's return to a mental institution. The Gossip Room was reverberating with all the news.

"I never was comfortable around Alma. She always seemed a little off, remember the time she dumped a bowl of soup on the waitress because she said it wasn't hot enough?" Rosy laughed. "Her bank account has protected her erratic behavior but attempted murder, well that was the final straw. I am relieved she is gone from here. I seem to be the only one who saw Bingo Bob kiss Sophia," she added.

"Are you sure? You said it was difficult to see from the window," Suzy Petuch challenged.

"Positive. It looked like he caught her off guard but she didn't seem to mind."

"Well, how about that? Will that bitch Sophia be joining us now that she is buddy buddy with Viola?"

Rosy asked the Crew. "Viola is off having lunch with Sophia instead of here with us."

"Calm down, Rosy, what's your problem with Sophia? She minds her own business and is always sociable," Suzy interjected.

"Rosy, a little jealous? Got your eyes on George," Esther Chaney added.

"Shut up, both of you. Sophia thinks she is better than we are," Rosy insisted.

The conversation turned to Lady Vikki. Ida took a sip of her chablis, "Vikki and Hans are getting it on more than usual, don't you think?"

"Vikki and Hans are shallow people, I don't trust either one of them."

"Wow, Rosy, is there anyone here you like?" Ida asked.

In a low voice Rosy described a conversation she overhead. "Lady Vikki was on her cell setting up a meeting in the City. I can't be sure but I thought at one point she mentioned Nazis."

"Oh, for God's sake, Rosy. You are a piece of work. What? Now you think Lady Vikki is a Nazi? Get a grip on your life," Suzy chided."There are no Nazis anymore."

CHAPTER 29

WILLOWIST

Sophia, Cat and George sat quietly, each stunned at the thought that Adolf Hitler was not only alive but was in a hospital bed a few hundred yards from where they were sitting.

Sophia spoke first. "Just remember, we are on our own on this mission and have strict instructions not to report back to anyone. Even with news like this. Although I have a feeling our superiors knew who was in that medical facility."

"What are we going to do?"

"Right now, lets just stay calm and analyze the situation. No one told us we would be extracting Adolph Hitler! Now I understand the reason this mission is so complicated and secret. It all makes sense now. Chancellor Becker and our President are concerned about the rise of the neo-Nazi movement. Franz Worthermann's increasing activities must mean he is going to use Hitler to ignite the Nazi movement. And its up to us to stop it."

"We have to take action soon," Cat said. "And I will personally kill that monster who was responsible for the death of her great grandfather," she thought but didn't say.

"George, you need to get us more details on Worthermann's plans. Are you hacked into anywhere you can do that?"

"I am still working on it Sophia."

George had configured his flat screen tv to be a secure computer screen.

"Tomorrow Worthermann is going to have a virtual meeting with some of his followers. I can hack into that and maybe we will see more details of his plans. I just have to be careful their security system doesn't alert them to my streaming connection, I do have the IP address hidden."

"Cat, you and I have to study these maps of the old cold war bomb shelter. That's going to be our only way into where the old Nazi, that is I mean Hitler, is being kept. We will need George to deactivate the alarm system and figure out how much time we will need to overpower the guard and get him out through the bomb shelter tunnel.

The helicopter will need to arrive at precisely the time we extract him. It's out of our hands then, we need to disappear. But the timing has to be exact. Chancellor Becker will arrest Worthermann and his aids for treason. There will be no mention of Adolf Hitler, Sophia surmised.

"It's crucial George have all the meeting places Worthermann set up for his Nazi followers whenever it is he is going to showcase Adolph Hitler. Again, not up to us but Interpol and the United States marshals will arrest the Nazi's on various criminal charges."

Cat expressed concern about Willowist residents. "Sophia, how do we know Worthermann doesn't have people embedded here to help carry out his plans."

"We don't. Just keep alert. I have been thinking about this and would normally think Worthermann would have planted the administrator. But we know Hans is in the Chancellor's camp, not Worthermann."

"Any other suspects?"

"Lady Vikki. Her father made a fortune with the help of the Third Reich. My bet is she reports to Worthermann or his top aide. Lets figure out how we can use her to send misinformation to the Nazis. Most important, we need to know Worthermann's timetable and be ready to move."

"Anyone else? I don't have anyone in mind?" Cat said.

Sophia replied: "Right now, anyone at Willowist except the three of us in this room could be a Nazi."

CHAPTER 30

MIAMI BEACH, FLORIDA

South Beach was colorful, lively and relaxing. Amsel relished this kind of assignment. Bikinis,sun,sand. Nothing compared to the gray skies he was used to in Hamburg. Even Angel was enjoying the Miami weather, although with his 200 plus poundage, high humidity days were brutal for him.

"Angel" was Emil Sebast. A former wrestler nicknamed Angel because he "sent people to Heaven" spent some time in prison for vicious assaults outside the ring, and he was recruited by Franz Worthermann to "sanitize" the Nazi movement. Get rid of major threats as they appear. When Worthermann wanted someone murdered, Angel was his weapon of choice.

Angel was a loyal member of Worthermann's killer squad and enjoyed the amenities that came with the position. Partying with attractive women, lots of beer, traveling in luxury sedans and private jets. When Angel appeared, death usually followed.

Amsel's investigation into Selingo catering led him to a boutique hotel near the South Beach hot spots for clubs and restaurants. He sipped on a German beer in the cafe off Collins Avenue and waited. The picture he had of Selingo's accountant showed a woman in her forties, brown hair brown eyes.

As Amsel relaxed, a few tables away JoJo Bissett adjusted her Maui Jim sunglasses and considered the situation. There were two bodyguards standing a few feet from Amsel, the number two man to Franz Worthington. And one of them was Angel! "This must be a big deal for him to be here," JoJo thought.

JoJo was not about to start a shootout and risk a lot of innocent tourists lives. Best to just wait and watch, she concluded. Amsel is obviously in South Beach for a reason, she concluded, and best to find out what the reason before killing him. And getting rid of Angel is the icing on the cake JoJo considered.

The Bri intelligence network had discovered Amsel was sent on a mission to South Beach, and JoJo followed him there to see what it was and then to eliminate him. She knew that would start a war with Worthermann and the High Command but the Bri plan was to disrupt the German militants from whatever they were planning with a neo-Nazi uprising.

Amsel signaled a woman to his table but JoJo was not with hearing distance.

"Mr. Amsel?," the lady extended her hand to him.

"Thank you for seeing me. I know you are on vacation but it's important we see the balance sheet and employee list for Selingo catering, did you bring it."

"Yes. Do you have what you promised me?"

Amsel handed the accountant a bag containing $100,000 in cash. JoJo could see a black duffel bag handed to the woman and a file folder handed to Amsel. The bodyguards seemed at ease but JoJo thought it better not to make a move on Amsel yet.

Amsel finished his beer, and he and the bodyguards walked down Collins Avenue and turned into a deserted dead end street. As JoJo followed, she saw them on cell phones and decided it was the perfect time and place to make her move. She drew her 9mm with silencer and heard a "pop." Surprised that Amsel didn't fall over, she felt a sharp pain in her chest. And then hands around her neck. As she coughed and saw blood squirting out she realized she had been shot. Her last view was of Angel Sebast choking her. JoJo Bisset of the Brie died on a dead end street in South Beach.

"Die, Bitch!" Amsel yelled at her dead body. He had recognized her from intelligence briefings and had led her to a place where he and Angel could kill her.

"Bisset was here but we took care of her," he said to Worthermann on his cell.

"The Bri think they are unbeatable, we are always one step ahead. Did you get the info on Selingo?"

"Yes, Sir. We have the names, addresses and family information on every one of Selingo's employees. Truck drivers. Cooks. Waiters, waitresses and bartenders. We even know their security codes and clearances to get into the football stadium."

"Good work. See you back here at headquarters. Don't get spoiled with the sun and those American women and make sure Angel doesn't get into a fight with any Americans,"Worthermann laughed.

"Tell Angel his next mission is in Paris, he can enjoy some of the French pastry once he rids us of that slut Tilly Miller," Worthermann added.

CHAPTER 31

HAMBURG

George hacked into the secure live webcast Worthermann set up for selected Nazi cells as Herr Worthermann called the meeting of his German military officers to order.

"Heil Hitler" each responded as the German conspirators went over their agenda. Worthermann explained there were many Nazi sympathizers worldwide but feared violent reactions from the international community for publicly declaring their allegiance to the proposed new Third Reich.

"Once we show the world new Nazi leadership, take over the German government, Nazi sympathizers will storm the governments in every country," Worthermann declared. "There will be no tolerance for any world leader against us, our people will not hesitate to remove enemies. Permanently."

Worthermann was a student of history and as much as he admired Adolf Hitler, he felt Hitler was a terrible military commander. The unexplained delays in attacking London during the early days of the war, especially when the weather was conducive to their air attack. The failure to see the Allies getting stronger. The attempt to fight on too many borders at once.

This time, Worthermann ruminated, this time it will be a coordinated effort to bring back the Third Reich. Not by unrealistic world military domination. Not by starting a war. Selected military targets.Selected political assassinations. Social media. Create worldwide chaos. Neo-Nazi cells coming out of hiding. He was convinced a large segment of the world public was tired of corrupt politics, tired of national media spinning the news the way of their own personal agenda. Tired of a few multinational wealthy corporate leaders manipulating the governments worldwide.People were ready for a structured, strong worldwide leadership. And who better than Herr Worthermann to step forth as the leader of the world. With a living Adolph Hitler by his side.

At the biggest media event in the world: halftime at the Super Bowl!

"Our Fuehrer will be taken to a secure facility in Philadelphia in a few days and then on Super Bowl Sunday we will move him into our suite at the stadium.

At halftime the world will see our Fuhrer is alive as my soldiers in Germany take over the German government, Nazi cells here and in Europe will come out of the shadows, and the world will witness the return of the Third Reich.

Arrangements have been made thanks to Nazi sympathizers that our delegation represents the German government and is to be treated as VIP's , with one of our founding members of the original Third Reich at our side."

He added he made arrangements to smuggle weapons and soldiers into the stadium but didn't disclose the details and how he had control of the Selingo security passes and food trucks.

Herr Worthermann alerted the group that there was successful infiltration into the administrations of Mayor Mike McCastle of Philadelphia and Mayor Jarrod Kitzen of NYC. On the word of the High Commander, McCastle and Kitzen would be assassinated, as would the German Chancellor, and the neo-Nazi groups would create chaos until Worthermann forces seized control. Worthermann's plan was once there was chaos, "thousands of our followers will come out of the shadows." The rise of the Third Reich would be complete. No one in the High Command questioned him.

"Heil Hitler" they saluted in unison.

CHAPTER 32

WILLOWIST

Sophia, George and Cat stared at the computer. No one said anything for a few minutes.

"Worthermann is deranged," Cat said. "A comatose murderer as his symbol of neo-Nazism? On second thought, that may be appropriate. A comatose symbol for a comatose movement!"

"Insane,"Sophia agreed. "We have to let our superiors know the exact location of the Nazi cells so arrests can be coordinated. If we are lucky, we could strike a death blow to the rise of Nazism worldwide. But remember, we are on our own for the extraction. Once we get Hitler, Worthermann's plan collapse, the Nazis will be arrested. Game over."

George was concerned. "We don't have our full game plan yet, Sophia. This is a dangerous situation, and if we get caught in the medical facility the mission fails. Not to mention what Worthermann will do to us. We have to time our extraction when Worthermann is in the States, and we can alert our superiors so they can order his arrest. The neo-Nazis awaiting Worthermann's announcement have to be arrested. The timing has to be perfect."

The three team members sat in agreement, each with their own concerns what happens if they fail to stop Worthermann. It could lead to the return of the Third Reich.

CHAPTER 33

"JoJo isn't answering her cell, Commander Fetterman," the corporal said.

"Keep trying, that's unlike her. I have seen her answer her cell with one hand while in a shootout with the other. What about her GPS tracker?"

"Nothing. She was at a cafe in South Beach, walked down Collins Avenue, turned a corner onto a dead end street and then the tracker went dead."

"No news on Amsel, did she dispose of him."

"Intelligence reports say he is alive and returned to Germany."

Fetterman considered the situation. "It's possible Amsel was on to her following him, surprised her and killed her. Check the police reports for South Beach, find out if any homicides."

"I did. All quiet except for the usual South Beach drugs and prostitution arrests."

"Keep monitoring Worthermann. Whatever he is up to in the States we have to beat him to it. And if he had JoJo killed I want to take care of Worthermann myself. He has declared war on us."

The mood at Bri headquarters was somber as the team realized JoJo may be dead.

CHAPTER 34

PARIS

"They know I'm here," Tilly nervously said to Chancellor Becker.

"Get out now and go to the coordinates I am texting you. I'll have someone get you to a safe place.

"Like this one! No. I am going to disappear on my own. Someone in your organization is feeding Worthermann information. They found me once, and they'll find me again if I take your help." Tilly threw the phone into the toilet to prevent anyone from using its GPS to track her location, changed into running clothes, put on a hoodie and sunglasses and left the apartment.

Becker was concerned. A leak in his inner circle? But who? He called in Brogan Fields.

"I want you to investigate who might be leaking information to Worthermann. Is there anyone new around her? A maid? A cook? A security guard? Brogan, someone around here can't be trusted. Find out who it is."

"I'm on it Boss." Fields thought to himself, "I'll tell Worthermann to have Angel take care of somebody here so I can put the blame on the deceased." Later that week, an aide to one of the Chancellor's cabinet members was riding his bicycle on a trail outside Berlin when he was shot and killed. A search of his apartment found information Brogan Fields had planted there falsely identifying him as the leak to Franz Worthermann. Chancellor Becker commended Fields for "finding that leak."

A few minutes after Tilly left her apartment she heard a blast in the area of the apartment.

"Just in time," she thought. "I got out just in time."

She bought a couple of burner phones.

"Hans, I can't talk long. Worthermann's men are after me. I will get in touch when I know I am safe."

Tilly reflected on her current situation. Once she was safely away from Worthermann's thugs, all would be good. Hans and she would retire to some beautiful island. "Politics. Politics just bring about disaster," she reflected. Tilly was sorry she got involved in Chancellor Becker's politics.

Tilly felt better that she was out of the apartment, no one was following her. Her relatives had a home outside of Toulouse, and she could hideout there until Hans was ready. Tilly felt relieved for the first time in weeks.

She heard the sound of a car coming up behind her on the sidewalk but didn't feel a thing when it hit her and sped away, leaving her lifeless body on the ground. Angel smiled at his handiwork as he continued driving toward the airfield where a jet was waiting for him.

CHAPTER 35

DEA agent Samuel "Sammy" Cusatis took a sip of his beer as he flicked through the pages of the report his field team had given him. Some of the tunnels in Tijuana that had moved contraband for years were found and closed off.

"Nice work," Sammy congratulated Confidential Informant 55. CI 55 had been a bodyguard for a Mexican druglord. Drugs were funneled into the States through a series of underground tunnels in Tijuana. CI 55 was captured by the DEA and at first refused to talk. "I am not a snitch", CI 55 had said. But when he heard his boss had a contract out on him, CI 55 was ready to make a deal with DEA for protection.

"Let's go over the situation. In return for your help in arresting members of the cartel who are using tunnels to enter the US from Mexico and more importantly, the location of the tunnels, you have been approved to enter the Witness Protection Program. Remember, the monies you received from illegal means have been forfeited, you can never again contact family or friends. You will be small business owner in South Dakota. The Witness

Protection program is secure. No one will be able to find you as long as you follow the rules. Never look back, never contact anyone from you past. You will have an apartment, a bank account and a job. Your new life will be much safer for you as long as you put your old life behind. I have to take this," Sammy interrupted his conversation with CI 55 to answer his cell phone.

"Sammy, long time, buddy, how are you?"

"Billy Green! Good to hear from you, what's up"

"We need to talk. I have some info to go over with you. I'm in D.C. so how about drinks tonight?"

Green and Cusatis sat in an English pub where agents for DEA, the CIA and FBI hung out. They waved hello to a few of their colleagues and settled into a booth. Nothing unusual about two friends having drinks together, no one paid any attention to them.

"Tacos and a pitcher of margaritas," Sammy said to the waitress.

"Must be all those assignments in Mexico," Billy Green laughed. "How's Pam?"

"Coming along. These treatments are wiping me out financially. Health care won't cover it all."

Sammy's teenage daughter was the victim of a drug dealer retaliating against one of Sammy's bigger drug busts. Shot several times she had been in a coma for months and eventually recovered except for residual paralysis. The rehab process was working but expensive.

"So what's new, Billy?"

"I need some information. It will be very much worth your time. I am looking for someone in the Program."

Sammy shook his head. "You know I can't do that. Not only is my job on the line, you know giving up the name of a Program participant leads to jail time. Besides, I don't have access once I accept the person and send them off. They become invisible to me."

Green changed the subject and talked some politics about the effect of increased border patrols on the illegal drug trade, and the antagonisms between the United States and Mexican governments over border issues, and politics in general.

"You're working Colombia, correct?" Sammy asked.

"Uh, huh," as Green downed his second margarita.

"El Gringo?"

"He's in the mix," Green answered.

"This isn't about him in any way, is it, Billy? He is the most vicious of all of them." Sammy didn't say it but he had heard the recent rumors, that Green was on the take and took orders from El Gringo.

Green put an envelope on the table and moved it toward Sammy. With all the agents in and out of the pub doing something in plain sight was less likely to get attention than trying to pass it under the table.

"All we need is a name and address. We'll never discuss it again. That envelope is yours and you'll get another one like it once we have the information."

"We, Billy? You, me and a druglord?"

Green ignored the reference and continued.

"Listen, you know in our line of work we have to deal with less than desirable people. The ends justifies the means, Sammy, you know that. We play with the druggies so we know how they work and then we get them. And besides, our government should have stepped in and helped pay for Pam's treatments. You are one of their best agents, and they let you down."

"No can do, Billy. Not happening. You know better than to try to bribe me," as Cusatis pushed the envelope back to Green. "It's none of my business but who do you want so badly anyway?" Longtime friends, Billy Green knew Sammy Cusatis would never turn him in for the attempted bribe. In reality, Billy Green considered Sammy may still accept it.

"Olivanti. Angelo Olivanti. El Gringo wants to meet him personally and have a little chat with him."

CHAPTER 36

WILLOWIST

Bingo Bob O'Donnell and Sophia took their what has become daily leisure stroll around the gardens.

"Bingo!," Bingo Bob O'Donnell laughed as they walked past a few Willowist residents.

"Bob, just curious, why do you shout so randomly?", Sophia questioned.

"Just my way of keeping things lighthearted around here. Some of the elderly residents get depressed", he observed. "And that in itself is surprising considering the opulent surroundings here."

Sophia didn't want to admit it to herself but she enjoyed spending time with Bingo Bob. His commitment to a healthy lifestyle and regular gym workouts were in line with her lifestyle. And he was handsome, she thought but never said. He was awakening feelings in her she tried to suppress.

Just like her evasiveness when people ask about her life before Willowist, Bob either changes the subject or vaguely talks about have some type of office job. Sophia suspected there was a more interesting story but no matter, she began to realize she had feelings for him. Feelings that had not been awakened since her days with James.

Likewise, Bingo Bob was the ladies man of Willowist, charming, handsome, outgoing. Women constantly tried to get his attention. It was Sophia that he felt comfortable with, it was Sophia he looked forward to seeing every day.

Bob was sure she did not have a physical relationship with George. "They seem more like work colleagues than in a relationship," he thought. "But why? Everyone here is retired. And what was up with Sophia and Viola Lepere. How did they know each other. They obviously had a falling out but suddenly they are friends?" Bob suspected there was a more interesting story about Sophia. Bingo Bob realized he was falling in love.

CHAPTER 37

RESTON, VA

DEA Agent Harry Cusatis took off his shoes and rubbed his feet. "Damn plantar warts." Cusatis had just returned from several days "in the cubicle", referring to DEA protocol mandates of a certain number of days of office work. He preferred visiting the field offices. Interviewing snitches who sought the protection of the United States government Witness Protection Program. Snitches who made money selling cocaine and heroin, destroying the lives of so many American young people. "They should be executed instead of given a new life courtesy of the taxpayers, including me."

Cusatis thought about his ex-wife and teenage children. Drug enforcement assignments put them in danger he knew because druglords extracted revenge and created fear by killing family members. But it was his constant unpredictable travel to places he couldn't tell Loreen about that strained his marriage. She wanted him out of the agency, and he loved her but it was his life.

He turned on tv in his temporary apartment and opened a bottle of Bud Lite. "Another exciting night as a recently divorced drug enforcement agent. So many of us choose the agency over family life. God knows why. Even if the druggies get caught, their lawyers get them plea deals. Deport the illegals but they just keep coming back. The US will never win a war on drugs, demand is through the roof.

"And that new American President won't let us do our jobs. Shit. His open borders are a godsend to the drug dealers. Venezuela, Colombia, Argentina. Everyone is sending their drugs into the US through Mexico. Its so open they aren't even using tunnels anymore. At least when Orangeman was President and started to build a wall, it suddenly became difficult for the illegal drugs to get to the American kids. Politics sucks," he ruminated.

The knock on his door reminded him how hungry he was. Tonight he ordered takeouts again from the closest Chinese restaurant. He grabbed two $20 bills, disturbed the delivery boy won't take credit cards.

As he opened the door, a burly Colombian man smashed his head with the door. Cusatis stumbled backward and fell onto the coffee table. He felt a needle go into his arm and then passed out.

It was the soaking humidity and heat that alerted Cusatis he was no longer in Reston. Cell phone, wallet, id papers nowhere to be found. Looking around he saw in was in a camp in the jungle. Colombia! This can't be good, he thought, adrenaline erasing the grogginess from the drugs and alerting him to danger.

"The boss will see you now," his big, burly companion grunted.

"Let's get right to it, Agent Cusatis,"El Gringo sneered. "I want information on someone in the Protection program."

"I don't have any." Cusatis started to say but he felt a huge pain from a fist thrust in his belly. Held by two men and facing El Gringo, Cusatis quickly considered his options. He had none.

"I will ask again Agent Cusatis. Before you answer, remember we know where your wife Loreen lives with Micky and Denise, your kids. And Pam. If you don't co-operate they and you will be pushing daisies, and you will die after you watch them die."

Cusatis tried to buy some time and think of how to get out of this situation."Who are you looking for?"

"Angelo Olivanti."

"How am I supposed to remember every snitch that goes into the Program."

Cusatis felt another blow to his stomach and a sharp cut on his face. He bellowed in pain.

"Get on this computer and get me that fucking information," El Gringo shouted. "And so you know my computer friend here has protected the IP address from being traced when you access the files."

Cusatis began to protest when he saw a picture of his daughter Pam on the computer. "Leave her alone!", he screamed.

Another blow this time to his kidney. Another scrape of a knife on his cheek.

"Is protecting some snitch worth the life of your own daughter," El Gringo sneered. Cusatis saw Angel staring at the picture of Pam.

He sat down and accessed the secure website. At first the screen said "you are not authorized to access this site."

"I can't access the site." Another hard punch to the stomach.

"We are wasting time.Next you lose an ear we will send to your daughter before Angel here pays her a special visit."

Thoroughly terrorized and resistance worn down, Cusatis kept scrolling through screens, entering passwords on each protected screen until he reached what El Gringo wanted to hear.

"Angelo Olivanti is now Bob O'Donnell. He is just listed as 'retired' and is at this retirement community. Some place in the States called Willowist. That's all I have."

Cusatis was saved from being tortured further and died quickly at Angel's hands.

CHAPTER 38

Commander Fetterman accessed the tracking device on JoJo's cellphone and confirmed that the last known location was a dead end alleyway in South Beach. Although her cellphone disappeared, their security system recorded any voice memos she made. Standard protocol in the Brie was to send voice messages to the secure site at headquarters during a mission. In the event the team member is killed or disappears, there will be information stored on the Bri secure computer.

Fetterman read the message to the other Bri team members:"South Beach. Have Amsel in sight. With bodyguard. Meeting with a woman and handing her an envelope. Can't hear discussion. Will follow Amsel and bodyguard and dispose of both."

"That's it, that's the full message," Fetterman announced. "She did send a picture of the woman. Our facial recognition software shows she is an accountant for various businesses. Find out what businesses she represents," Fetterman ordered the Bri tech member. "Most likely a drug deal going down, and we can score points with DEA if we send that info along to them. A psycho-path associate of El Gringo named Angel is there and that doesn't bode well for JoJo.

Fetterman surmised Amsel knew he was being fol-lowed and that he and Angel took JoJo by surprise and either kidnapped her or murdered her. Sadly, he consid-ered there was no reason to think she was kidnapped, there have been no demands.

"I think JoJo is dead, my friends. What business is that accountant tied to."

"Just a catering business called Selingo's and several small businesses in Pennsylvania," the tech found with a quick internet search. "Nothing that looks like a neo-Nazi operation."

"Check out that Selingo's. Although I don't know why Franz Worthermann and his followers would have any interest in a catering business. Once Worthermann is out of his safe house in Germany we'll get him. We are going to the States! Worthermann won't know what hit him.

CHAPTER 39

The Swoop Sisters were ecstatic. The Eagles were advancing to the Super Bowl, and this was to be their last football party of the year at Willowist.

"What about the guest list for the suite. This will be the toughest yet, who to invite," Mary Margret noted.

The Swoops had maintained a list of Willowist residents who were hardcore Eagles fans and rotated them, taking turns to be invited to the suite the Swoops had for every home game.

"Sophia, George, Cat, Bingo Bob for sure. And Viola since she and Sophia are friends again." For this game they set up a lottery system for Willowist residents who were interested in going to the stadium.

"We'll make sure the people who don't get to come with us have a first class party here at Willowist,"Mary Margret smiled.

Their game day plan was to have the Willowist van take the group to the stadium and access the suite long before the stadium doors officially opened. The Swoops always had special privileges.

"Here's a list of goodies for the suite. Add anything you want and then call that new caterer, Selingo's I think. Remind them we have our orders filled before the stadium doors open", Lizzie said.

Lizzie and Sophia had become close. "And make sure there is some Fabian music playing for Sophia's benefit."

"Of course. I love Sophia too," Mary Margret added. "This is one Super Bowl that will go down in history."

CHAPTER 40

WILLOWIST

Bicycles were rarely used at Willowist, although Bingo Bob donated several racing bikes and occasionally rode on the two lane country road, remembering his younger days doing biathlons. He used to love the run, bike, run races and often beat competitors much younger.

Bob invited Sophia for a bike ride through the country about ten miles each way. "There's a state park, I asked the cooks to make us sandwiches, they're in my backpack."

Sophia, who had been in combat in Afghanistan and Iraq, pretended to be concerned about a bike ride in the country. "These bike lanes are not safe! So many people are driving distracted with texting and all that," she laughed.

" I will look out for you. You bring the bottle of wine. The government gives grants to communities to create bike lanes for people," Bob replied.

"Government grants. Ha. That's our taxpayer money to begin with," Sophia said. "We pay taxes, the government gives us a paltry portion back and makes it look like they are doing us a favor."

Bob laughed, "A little cynical today, aren't you Sophia? Especially for a former state department employee."

Sophia and Bob enjoyed each other's company and both were developing feelings for the other, although Sophia was fighting it. They took turns being the lead bike and enjoyed the deserted country road.

Neither one paid attention to the sound of the helicopter getting louder until it was only about 100 yards from them. The helicopter hovered over them briefly, then sped away. It turned around and headed back their way.

"You don't see many of those around here," Bod pointed out. "That's odd. It seems to be buzzing us. Look it's landing right over there, on the grassy field."

Sophia noticed it first. Two Colombians jumped out and the metal of their guns sparkled in the sunlight. "Come with us Olivanti, and you won't be hurt!," one of the men screamed.

"Bob! Follow me!" Sophia and Bob dropped their bikes and ran toward a wooded area, hearing gunshots.

Both fell on the ground and took out handguns from their backpacks and fired back. After a brief shootout Sophia hit one of the men, killing him while Bob wounded the other who quickly limped back toward the helicopter. Bob's backpack had been hit, knocking him over. Sophia quickly went to his side.

"Bingo!" Bob shouted in the direction of the helicopter. "I'm ok, my backpack took the bullet. But the sandwiches are ruined," he said to Sophia.

Cat was reviewing info on neo-Nazis with George and grabbed her car keys when she received Sophia's frantic call for help." By the time she arrived, Sophia and George were shaken but peddling back.

Cat gave Sophia a quick glance, and Sophia's reaction let Cat know not to say anything. Safely back in George's apartment, Sophia and Bob said to each other almost in unison "You have a gun in your backpack?"

CHAPTER 41

SOMEWHERE OVER THE UNITED STATES

The helicopter was returning to a deserted airfield where a jet would take the pilot and the wounded man back to Colombia. The druglords and their men flew in and out of the States easily, going low and under the radar. They had arranged for strategically placed private airfields that could handle small jets. Billy Green made sure the drug cargos were not confiscated by authorities.

"I hope we didn't hurt him too bad," The wounded man said to the helicopter pilot. "We're fucked if we did. El Gringo wants to take care of this guy himself."

Wounded man called El Gringo. "You took care of business?", the druglord asked.

"There was a problem, Boss. He was with a woman and they both had guns and fucked us up. The woman damn well knew how to use a firearm and killed Bario and hit me."

"You idiot! I'll put a bullet in your head," El Gringo screamed and slammed the phone down. "An old woman and an old man beat you up and kill Bario, one of my best men!

The only way to take care of Olivanti is for me to come to the States to do it," El Gringo shouted.

CHAPTER 42

WILLOWIST

"Sophia. Thank you! You saved my life! But you are not some desk employee at the State Department the way you handled that weapon."

Sophia's first thought alarmed her. Did Worthermann know of their mission? Is Cat in danger? George?

"Why don't you tell me what's going on? Who is Olivanti? Did they mistake you for someone else? You invite me for a quiet bicycle ride in the country secretly carrying a handgun in your backpack. Suddenly a helicopter shows up and some thugs jump out and scream the name Olivanti? And starts shooting at us? Who were those guys? You obviously know how to handle a weapon.Lots of questions for you, Bob. If that's really your name."

Bob knew his witness protection cover was exposed, and that El Gringo knew who he was and where he was. Bob made the decision to confide in Sophia. After all, he thought, she fought side by side with him and saved his life. He quietly told Sophia about his military experience, his undercover work and his involvement in breaking up

a major drug cartel. He explained how his friend, prosecutor Darrough was murdered in a case Bob had worked
on. " I don't know how they found out where I am but
you and Cat may be in danger too after what happened
today. Best guess its El Gringo, the Colombian druglord.
He won't stop until he finds me!"

"Bob, you have to get in touch with your government contact and get reassigned into the program.
Today! And they need to find who leaked your name and
location." Neither knew at that point that Agent Cusatis
gave him up and was now dead.

"No. I am not leaving you. When we are all at the
Super Bowl I am going to ask you to marry me."

"Marry? Sophia shook her head in disbelief. And ignored Bob's questions about who she was and why she
was at Willowist. She was not about to compromise her
mission. This was not the first nor would it be the last
shootout she would have to deal with. Adolph Hitler is
on life support a few hundred yards away, and Bob talking about marriage antagonized her.

CHAPTER 43

Hans was exhausted. "Being administrator with all these old farts and their demands is hell," he sighed. "I have to step up my plans to leave." He relaxed as he thought of life with Tilly and took a sip of his Beck. "Nobody makes beer like Germany!"

Hans was aware Chancellor Becker had political trouble brewing with the growing popularity of neo-Nazism and Franz Worthermann, and he was determined to he jump ship if Becker was ousted. Hans was allied with Becker but that was when the Chancellor's political fortune was on the rise. Loyalty was not a word anyone would associate with Hans Hansberger.

The question on his mind was "when." When would Becker be out and that Nazi Worthermann be in Hans considered. "Worthermann will never trust me, given my relationship with Becker," Hans mused. "And if I renounce Becker I will have no allies. If Becker can just hang on a few more months I'll have enough money hidden away for a life with Tilly." Hans had not yet discovered his Panamanian account with money he embezzled from the Willowist residents was locked. Interpol was ready to arrest Hans as soon as he tried to access the money, confirming it was his account.

His thoughts were interrupted by Rosy DeStefano. "Oh God, one of that awful Crew. No matter what I do they will rip me apart in the Gossip Room."

"Administrator Hansberger," Rosy began, "I had a routine physical by the Willowist doctor, and he won't take my medicare."

"I'll take care of it. As we discussed many times, the money comes automatically out of your Willowist bank account, the bill you get shows that you have no additional payment, not even for the office visit." Hans thought but didn't say: "You old hag. How stupid are you, I have gone over that a thousand times with you."

As Rosy was leaving, Lady Vikki entered Hans' office. Rosy nodded knowingly and left the room."Why didn't you wait until that stupid old lady left? You know she will be telling everyone you and I are fucking in the middle of the day."

"Calm down. I just wanted to tell you Bingo Bob had some injuries. He apparently was mugged on a bike ride."

"Mugged? On a country road? Did some farmer run him over with a tractor?'

"I don't know Hans, you don't have to be sarcastic. I know you are too busy embezzling the residents money to know whats going on, was just trying to inform you so you could check up on him" as she stormed out of the office.

"I can't wait until Worthermann lets me dispose of this idiot! It won't be much longer I have to play footsies with him. It's for the benefit of the Third Reich," she kept reminding herself.

Hans called Bob O'Donnell's apartment faking concern for Bob. Hans was good at hiding his dislike for the residents. "The old farts" as he referred to them in private.

"Bob, what happened? I heard you were mugged. You ok?", Hans questioned. "You can't trust anybody anymore."

"Boy, that's an understatement," Bob replied. "I am ok, just a little shaken up."

Thanks to the intervention of Sophia's superiors there was no mention of the helicopter attack on Bob and Sophia in the news.

"Listen, if there is anything I can do for you, just let me know," Hans lied. "We aren't going to mention this to the others, I don't want to cause panic." Hans was more concerned about any publicity about Willowist. He was close to finding Tilly and absconding with the embezzled money to some Greek Island to live "happily ever after" as he had promised her. Yes, he thought, better if the residents don't know about the mugging. The less attention on this the better.

The Gossip Room was already reverberating with news that Bob and Sophia were off for a tryst in the state park and some cocaine addicts mugged them for drug money. Sophia thought it best to start that rumor before the real story is discovered.

CHAPTER 44

BERLIN

Chancellor Becker was livid that Tilly had died. He was certain it was murder and that somehow Franz Worthermann was behind it. A hit and run. While walking on the sidewalk! No witnesses of course. The Paris police not bothering to investigate.

Becker expressed concern at his cabinet meeting that "something was going on" with the Nazi sympathizers. He was alerted by his security team he might be the victim of a coup attempt but didn't want to call attention to his fears.

"We are keeping close watch on any Nazi gatherings and will make arrests once my police finish their investigation. The 'suspicion of a riot' law will get them off the streets for awhile."

"What about the High Command? Are they involved?" the Defense Secretary asked.

"If they engage in any type of treasonous activity they will be arrested," Chancellor Becker assured his Cabinet.

"Even Franz Wortherman," the Defense Secretary asked incredulously.

"If Franz is involved, yes, even Franz Worthermann. "If you see or hear anything, just let Brogan know. He can be trusted."

CHAPTER 45

WILLOWIST

"Let's go over the plan," Sophia began. She, Cat and George were in George's apartment, and he had all his tech equipment set up.

"I heard the Swoops have a great menu for their final party," George said.

"Stay focused, George! Forget the party, we are talking about the completion of our mission," Sophia chided him. "Timing is everything from here on out. One mistake, and the mission is compromised. As well as our safety."

"Cat and I will enter the medical research building in the early morning hours of Super Bowl Sunday and remove our target."

"Just say it, Sophia. We are going to capture Adolf Hitler!," Cat exclaimed.

"Yes, Cat, its Hitler. George will inject a temporary sleeping med through the vents which will temporarily sedate all the Germans while, we wear gas masks and remove Hitler into a waiting ambulance where Cat will stay with him. When Worthermann shows up at the medical facility to get Hitler he will be detained and arrested for various crimes by Homeland security and ICE who will be hiding in the woods and who will secure the airport.fHitler will be taken to Germany, and whatever Chancellor Becker does with him is no concern for us. Mission accomplished, and we quietly leave Willowist. This mission is wearing me out, I may really retire!"

"Are we at least going to the Super Bowl," George interjected.

"George! You are a tech nerd, tech nerds don't follow football," Cat commented.

"Oh yes we do. And I love the Jets. Too bad I have to be here to coordinate the drones and monitors. But I will have a tv on so I can watch the game."

"It figures. The Jets. You are the only guest at Willowist that likes the Jets," Cat laughed.

Sophia added, "We have to go to the Super Bowl and be at the suite. In case anything goes wrong we have to disrupt Worthermann's halftime plans. If things go right, the Nazi cells, Nazi workers in the Willowist facility will all be arrested at the same time. If we are lucky no one will know there was a plan to have Adolph Hitler at the Super Bowl, as incredible as that sounds. Plans have been made that our weapons will be in the stadium for us.

So here's how it goes, we go in and get Hitler out in the early morning hours of Super Bowl Sunday. When Worthermann shows up he will be arrested. At the same time the Nazi gatherings awaiting what Worthermann called his "big surprise" at halftime will all be arrested by US and Interpol agents for domestic terrorism and other charges.

Then the three of us go our separate ways and disappear into whatever our next mission is," Sophia summarized.

"What about Bingo Bob and you," George said softly. He suppressed his own feelings for Sophia and wanted her to be happy.

"Oh George. You know I don't get involved with colleagues," Sophia replied somewhat sadly.

Sophia and Cat told George the story of Angelo Olivanti entering the witness protection program and changing his identity to Bingo Bob.

"I did all I could, George, to encourage Bob to get out of here and into a new protection program. But he said the druglord found him once and will find him again. Bob wants to stand his ground and get this over with one way or another."

"George, if you see any activity on El Gringo or his thugs coming here for Bob, we need to alert him," Sophia continued. "I begged him to leave Willowist immediately but he will be at the party and the game. Let's hope our mission is successful, and no one ever knows what might have happened."

George and Cat agreed and continued working on their plans.

CHAPTER 46

Billy Green was relieved he was off the hook about finding Angelo Olivanti now that El Gringo knew Olivanti's witness protection identity was Bingo Bob O'Donnell at a retirement home in the States call Willowist. Green hoped his part in this process was over. He has enough money to retire comfortably but he also knows once you are "in the business" of illegal drugs, you never get out.

"Boss, you can't expect me to interfere with the Witness Protection program! I don't even know how it works. Protecting your business deals at the Miami ports is one thing but hell, the Witness Protection program?"

"Shut up moron! You haven't had any problem protecting drug shipments, you're already in this pretty deep," El Gringo bellowed."

"Yeah, but the people I eliminated were low-level drug dealers, not someone protected by the United States government."

"I am going to take care of this snitch myself but you will be with me, got it?"

El Gringo took a sip of his aguardiente and barked orders to one of his henchman: "get my jet ready, we are going to the States. I am going to pay a visit to Willowist. Olivanti will be sorry he crossed me."

El Gringo had several jets, and his pilots knew how to fly under the radar. They routinely entered and exited foreign countries without detection and had private airstrips available. "Money talks, nobody walks" was El Gringo's motto, which helped him build a network of corrupt politicians, customs officers, seaport vessel traffic controllers and a host of others that are willing to let the illegal drug trade flourish. Money and terrorism were El Gringo's two biggest weapons.

When an anti-drug organization tried to establish a presence near the Miami ports where suspected contraband ended, their leaders died in an explosion of "undetermined origin". When the Chief of Police in a Venezuelan town ordered a crackdown on drugs, his lifeless body was found hanging on a pole in front of the police station. Even an anti-drug Catholic priest was found murdered in his Venezuelan parish office, cocaine spread all over his body.

"You have to kidnap Olivanti O'Donnell or whatever the hell his name is and bring him to me. My pilot found an old airfield next to this Willowist place. I can't go walking around some old people home. It's obvious I am not an old shithead. I don't look like some old idiot. Do I?"

"No Boss, you don't. All right. I'll come up with a story for the Administrator. There has to be a reason a DEA official is at a retirement community without causing havoc and my supervisors hearing about it."

"You are a good liar, this one will be easy for you. And don't worry, this one you don't have to get your hands dirty. I am going to personally bring this snitch back here on the plane and make sure he dies a slow, painful death. I spent time in prison because of him, lost millions because of him. We'll land at that airstrip near where he is living, and you bring him to me."

"Do you have a recent picture of him, Boss?"

Idiot! What do I pay you for? You find him at Willowist and bring him to the plane. Otherwise you are useless to me."

Green knew what that meant. When someone was declared "useless" to El Gringo, they never were seen again. "I just have to find out what he looks like and where he is," Billy Green thought to himself.

CHAPTER 47

WILLOWIST

It was 3 pm when Laura Moser became the first resident in line for the final Swoop Sisters' Super Bowl party the Friday before the Sunday game. Johnny Nelmes aided by his walker was next. The excitement generated by the Swoops over the Philadelphia Eagles being the first team ever to play in the Super Bowl at its own stadium was spreading throughout the retirement campus.

The Swoops weren't ready for the partygoers and were surprised the line started two hours before the doors were to open.

"Lizzie, we have to do something! Some of those people in line have walkers, wheelchairs, are really old. What will do if they start fainting or falling over?" Mary Margret was concerned.

"I'll call the kitchen and tell them to speed up getting the buffet set up, you call Hans and tell him we need staff to offer water and chairs to the people in line. We'll open the doors as early as we can," Lizzie added.

Hans was not happy when he received Mary Margret's phone call.

"What do you want me to do? I can't chase the people away?"

But Hans knew if anyone was seriously ill or hurt because of standing in line it would all come back on him.

"Ok, ok. I'll get our staff to work it all out," Hans relented. There were many other places he would rather be, like in Tilly's bed, he thought.

Except for 91 year old Betty Ulshafer passing out while standing in line there were no incidents by the time the Swoops got the doors open at 4 pm, a full hour before the planned time. Hans had a paramedic and two nurses assigned to the party and hoped no one would need them. Betty was revived and ready to party.

The partitions were removed, and the party room was huge. The Sisters had decorated the walls with pictures of Eagles, the stadium and of them posing with various football players. There were green and white streamers and balloons in honor of the color of their uniforms for the big game. Even the DJ they hired used to work for a radio station that carried the Eagles games live.

Food was plentiful, and a similar menu to what a smaller group of residents would enjoy at the game in the Swoops' private suite. Philly cheesesteaks. Scrapple. Pretzels. The Swoops also had foods available less disruptive of the residents who were on medications and who had sensitive digestive systems.

"Remember when Natalie Simpson had to be taken to the ER when she had a bad reaction to the cheesesteaks," Lizzie had reminded Mary Margret when they were planning the menu.

The song list included Philly oldie favorites such as doo-wop, the Jive Five, Dion and the Belmonts, Ronettes, Crystals and of course the "Bobbys", as Sophia called them. Bobby Rydell. Bobby Darin. Bobby Vinton. The Swoops made sure Fabian songs were added for Sophie.

Every seat at every table was filled, as well as the seats along the walls. Arlene Cantnor was one of the first to start dancing. Her version of the Bristol Stomp was in slow motion but it ignited a rush of residents to the dance floor.

It was Bobby Vinton's "Too Fat Polka" that put the nurses on high alert. While the men sat around the tables, the ladies took to the dance floor. Miram Longnecker and a well revived Arlene Cantnor flew around the dance floor, top polka speed. Some of the older dancers still remembered their polka steps, just at a slightly slower pace. Even the usually cynical Crew members joined the fun. When the DJ replayed the song everyone formed a circle and clapped their hands while Sophia and Viola showed their polka moves. The nurses sighed with relief there were no injuries,and the DJ slowed the dance music down with Frank Sinatra's version of "When I Fall in Love".

Bingo Bob was relentless in asking Sophia to dance, and she eventually agreed. Sophia had encouraged George and Cat to attend the party to avoid attention on their absence. George's eye started twitching when Arlene asked him to a slow dance. Cat enjoyed the company of 94 year old WWII veteran Patrick Taylor. She loved hearing the stories of the battlefield.

Mary Marconi and Dr. Anthony Stram were the hit of the stroll. They were as graceful in their 80's as they were in their teens. Becky Tamellini and Theodore Aster took a microphone and sang along with the recording of Love is Strange by Mickey and Sylvia. Elvis Presley, Buddy Holly, The Crests all led to singalongs by the residents.

"Let them have fun tonight because in 48 hours this place will go up in flames with them in it," Lady Vikki thought but didn't say. "Heil Hitler" she mumbled under her breath. Hans put his arm around her waist, confirming the Gossip Room rumors they are a couple. "And this idiot and his friend Becker will be shot at about the same time," she thought to herself as she looked at Hans with an enticing smile. "God, how I hate this whiny excuse for a man." Lady Vikki cursed her assignment to use sex to keep Hans under her control.

"Just give me a chance, Sophia. Let's see how it goes," Bob whispered to Sophia as they were dancing to A Million to One by Jimmy Charles.

"Bob, I told you, I am not interested in a relationship. I value your friendship but that's where it stays.

"But why? I know you have feelings for me. I can tell."

"No, Bob. It's called friendship and you need to circulate around the room. A lot of the ladies here would jump at the chance to dance with you."

Sophia returned to the table with George and Cat. They agreed at this point it wouldn't jeopardize the mission if they were seen together. "We need to sleep in tomorrow, go over our plans one more time. Tomorrow night we make our move."

"Do you think Lady Vikki is suspicious we have something going on?", Cat asked Sophia.

"I think she did but as days went by she moved on to other things. She is up to something though."

"She has been active on her satellite phone. I still haven't been able to hack into all the conversations but the calls are all traced to Germany. Many of those calls are to the direct line we know belongs to Franz Worthermann, and it appears his soldiers will pick up Hitler at 7 a.m. on Sunday," George noted.

"We'll have Hitler on his way to Chancellor Becker by then, " Cat said. "When will Worthermann be arrested?"

"He will be arrested at the facility next door, and returned to Germany where Chancellor Becker's top aide, Brogan Fields is making the arrangements to have Worthermann charged with treason. I am sure the powers that be will make sure something happens to Worthermann, they won't let there be a public trial giving him the chance to be in the media on the world stage. Don't be surprised if another inmate murders Worthermann in jail," Sophia explained.

"You three look like you could need some food," Lizzie interrupted as she brought a tray of wine and cheeses to their table. "Our bus will leave here Sunday morning at 7 am. Game time is 6 pm but we will have access to our suite hours before the stadium opens to the general public."

"Must be nice to have friends in high places," Cat laughed.

"We are so happy you three are coming!", Lizzie answered.

"I have to cancel out, family issues that need attention," George lied. The issues that needed attention revolved around electronic eavesdropping on the Germans and providing location information to backup if

Sophia and Cat are exposed to trouble. George was responsible to know when and where Franz Worthermann was and to give the law enforcement agents who will be hidden in the woods the signal to swarm in and make the arrest. Timing was important in this operation.

Once Adolf Hitler was in Sophia and Cat's control, things would move fast. US agents and Interpol agents will be in position to arrest the major neo-Nazi cells, followed by a joint news release from the United States President, German Chancellor Becker and the France President saying an attempt by the neo-Nazis to engage in violent terrorism in efforts to revive the Third Reich has failed. No mention will be made of Adolf Hitler. George didn't care what the Germans did with Hitler. He just wanted the mission to go smoothly without any casualties of innocent people.

"Well, I hope you get to watch the game on television at least. The cameras usually pan to our suite at least once during the game, and we all get to wave to a worldwide audience," Mary Margret offered.

By 9 pm the last remaining residents thanked the Swoops and ambled off to their rooms.

Lady Vikki and Hans would have one last night of lovemaking. Several residents found a mate for the evening, the women hoping the viagra would excite their men enough for a few hours of fun. Bingo Bob left alone after being gently rebuffed by Sophia yet he still planned on asking her to marry him at the Super Bowl.

Sophia, Cat and George went to their apartments. Each one had been involved in dangerous missions and this one caused more of the adrenaline rush of undercover work than any other.

CHAPTER 48

Franz Worthermann boarded his private jet with six heavily armed soldiers with a scheduled arrival time at Willowist about 12 am Super Bowl Sunday. His jet was preceded by another jet with 6 more soldiers and weapons. Flying low over the States to avoid radar, the soldiers would be dropped off at the abandoned airstrip a few miles from Willowist. Several would plant explosives around the Willowist building, ready to be detonated by Lady Vikki on Worthermann's signal. The Germans working in the medical research building will be evacuated and flown back to Germany.

The other soldiers were to be transported quietly to the Selingo warehouse where they would confiscate the security passes and uniforms of Selingo employees and load weapons alongside the food to be delivered to the stadium. Angel would be in charge while Worthermann left for the stadium.

An ambulance will have Hitler and the medical equipment parked at a back entrance to the stadium. Once the Selingo trucks arrive, the food will be distributed to stadium employees unaware the Germans had replace the Selingo people. The suite Franz Worthermann had a German company reserve for the game would become known in history as the place where the Third Reich was reborn!

At the exact moment Worthermann unveils a living, although comatose, Adolf Hitler, Brogan Fields would assassinate Chancellor Becker. Nazi cells in several United States, German and France cities would create chaos and topple the governments.

Worthermann settled into his seat and took a sip of German beer. "I have waited all my life for this moment," he reflected. "The New World Order will be under my control. Heil Hitler!"

CHAPTER 49

CALI, COLOMBIA, FRIDAY, SUPER BOWL WEEKEND

EL Gringo shouted to his most trusted bodyguard Mikali for the trip to the States, "Clean your weapons and get ready to leave. Load the weapons on my jet."

To avoid terrorizing the residents and having someone call 911, Mikali, a one man murder machine, would pose as a delivery man and ask to speak to Administrator Hans. Once in Hans office, Mikali would use his usual power of persuasion to force Hans to have Bingo Bob O'Donnell report to his office.

Bob would then be taken to the airfield where El Gringo would "welcome" him on the plane. Once in Colombia El Gringo planned a long, slow painful death for Angelo Olivanti now known as Bingo Bob O'Donnell. "Snitches are the lowest form of life on the earth," El Gringo told his men time and time again.

CHAPTER 50

WILLOWIST, SUPER BOWL SATURDAY 2 PM

Sophia, Cat and George huddled in George's apartment to finalize their plans. George was monitoring the Nazi cells, noting that there was "no activity to be concerned about." He was unaware that Brogan Fields overhead conversations George and Chancellor Becker had about the surveillance. Fields alerted Worthermann, and the renegade Germans set up a sophisticated blocking system and alternative communication system between the High Command and each individual Nazi cell. George was out of the loop on Worthermann's plans.

"About 3 am Cat and I will enter the bomb shelter from the woods. We'll use the plastic explosive device to open the door to the research building. The noise will awaken the Nazis, and we will dispose of them," Sophia explained. "We'll get Hitler back through the bomb shelter to the airstrip, and off he goes to Chancellor Becker, and our mission is done."

"But we still have to go to the Super Bowl?"

"Yes, Cat. Just in case anything goes wrong. Weapons will have been stored in the closet area just outside the suite. Once all is ok, we come back here, gather our things and go our separate ways."

"I am going to miss you two," Cat sighed, as George's eye twitched.

"Who knows? Maybe we'll get another mission together, Cat. It's been great fun getting to know you both," Sophia replied.

Cat acknowledged her respect for Sophia, "You are an amazing woman, Sophia! You have been through so much and are so highly trained. I feel safe with you. And if I can look as good as you when I'm in my 40's let alone 60's, I will be a happy girl."

"Well, I will miss you both also."

Even George managed to add "I am pleased to work with such professionals."

The trio felt confident this mission would end peaceably and efficiently.

CHAPTER 51

TEL AVIV, SUPER BOWL WEEKEND

"It's confirmed. He will be at the stadium for the Super Bowl," Commander Fetterman announced to his team. "I want to be there and see the look on his face before we put 3 bullets in the head of Franz Worthermann. Not only for dealing a major blow to the neo Nazis but also as payback for when he had JoJo murdered. I am sure Angel will be there too, I want to personally take him out."Fetterman added, "How do we get into the stadium?"

"That's a problem. Tickets are impossible to get.We'll have to intercept Worthermann on his way to the game," Jim Mason replied. "We don't know where or when he will get in the States but we have arranged a commercial flight for you and several men. Our United States operatives will have weapons and pick you up. By then we should know more about Worthermann's travel plans."

"Send a couple of men to Selingo Catering, that connection puzzles me why Worthermann showed so much interest. I still regret sending JoJo to Miami, she would still be alive if I hadn't. She didn't find out why

Worthermann's men were interested in Selingo. Maybe its nothing, maybe its important. Let's cover all bases."

Fetterman and his team weren't aware that Adolph Hitler was alive. They knew Worthermann had some grand plan to ignite what he referred to as "the return of the Third Reich." The Bri team believed this was their chance to strike a death blow to Nazism as well as take out the leader of the German High Command.

Fetterman was neutral on Becker's leadership and had no antagonism to the United States. In fact, he was grateful to leaders in both countries for surreptitiously alerting the Bri when former Nazis were found and delaying making an arrest to give the Bri a chance to dispose of them. Just last month Fetterman's team raided a house in the canyons of Hollywood.

The estate on Cielo Drive, the infamous street actress Sharon Tate lived on when murdered by the Charles Manson gang, housed two former concentration camp officers. Both in their 90's, a wealthy movie celebrity had made their living arrangements.Fetterman often referred to celebrities known to be Nazi sympathizers as "Hollywood Hypocrites." After several quiet years with 24/7 nurses and regular maid service, there was no longer need for security at the Cielo Drive mansion, and the Bri made their move.

Fetterman and three of the Bri dressed in full SWAT uniforms climbed a rear fence. Security lights lit up the yard like a football stadium at night. Using a silencer Fetterman shot out the lights, and the team quickly ran through the manicured gardens to the side of the house. They used a handheld device to tap into the security system and deactivated it.

One of the nurses was making tea in the kitchen and dropped the cup on the floor when she saw the Bri team enter the kitchen area. Fetterman locked her in the laundry room area with a warning she and her family would be murdered if she reports anything she saw and heard. He didn't approve of killing innocent people, telling his team "that would make us just as evil as the Nazis."

The two German officers were near death on their own but the Bri speeded up the process by putting 3 bullets in each the head of each German. The wealthy celebrity, upon hearing the news of the death of the Germans, left for Europe with no forwarding address. She was no longer interested in helping former Nazis and resolved to stay out of politics.

Commander Fetterman shook off the memories and focused on the present. "We will get Worthermann this time! He has managed to evade us for years but his time has come," Fetterman told his team.

CHAPTER 52

SELINGO RESIDENCE, EARLY MORNING HOURS SUPER BOWL SATURDAY

Barry Jr. awoke with a start when a large hand was placed over his mouth. What looked to be a giant man terrified Junior, and Junior felt pee in his pajama pants.

"Keep quiet or I will kill you," Angel whispered. "If I take my hand out of your mouth, will you keep quiet? Or do you want to die?"Sobbing, Barry, Jr, with wide eyes staring at Angel shook his head yes. Angel took Junior to the van and drove away.

A few hours later the radio awoke Barry Selingo with an early morning traffic report on KYW radio. "What time is it?", his wife asked. "3 am. I have to get to the warehouse to get everything ready for tomorrow's game. We need to be at the stadium by 5 am on Sunday." He kissed his wife on the check and left the house.

At the warehouse a few hours Barry realized he had left his cell in his car. There were 48 missed calls from his wife! "Honey, sorry, my cell was in the car." Shrieking, crying, screaming she told him Junior was missing. "Calm down. Maybe he is in the game room or went over to a friends. Hold on, I am getting a call from an un-known number, maybe its Junior."

Barry stood straight up,stunned to hear a deep voice. "Junior is safe and will be returned to you after you do what we say. If you call the police or do anything but what we tell you, his throat will be slit." Angel enjoyed conversations like this. Terrorizing someone early in the morning meant it was going to be a good day.

"Some men will be at the warehouse, do everything they say. Got it."

In a shaken voice, Barry replied "got it." Barry lied to his wife that Junior was at a friends and would be back later in the day.

Even if Barry didn't cooperate several of his employ-ees were visited by Worthermann's men and given huge amounts of money to turn over their uniforms and secu-rity badges to the Germans.

Like it or not, Selingo catering was going to aid the rise of the Third Reich.

CHAPTER 53

WILLOWIST, SUPER BOWL SUNDAY 9 A.M.

Bingo Bob O'Donnell carefully looked over the diamond ring he had purchased. He was certain Sophia was in love with him, and he was certain she would agree to marry him. Bob reflected on the last several weeks, the quiet walks, conversations and gym workouts with Sophia. He was in love, and the feeling was wonderful. Bob smiled, absolutely nothing could ruin this beautiful day.

The vibration on his cell startled him from his thoughts of Sophia.

"Bob, can you come to my office for a minute," Hans asked. "It's important." *There is a foreign looking man holding a gun to my head, looking for you,* Hans thought as he left a message on Bingo Bob's cell phone.

Earlier that morning Hans was readying his computer files and documents for his escape from Willowist. He decided Super Bowl Sunday was the perfect day for him to leave forever. Once he was safely in France he would search out Tilly.

Hans thought it best to transfer some of his Panamanian account to a new French account. His contact for money laundering, Shelia Fromme hasn't returned his calls but he had the account numbers. Hans typed in his screen name, code, password and special secret words. ACCESS DENIED. "I must have typed wrong. Several tries later, same result. Access Denied.

Sheila Fromme not returning his calls. Access denied to his Panamanian accounts. "I have to stay calm". Hans tried his Switzerland account. Slightly less money but it would get him to France, and he would sort things out with Fromme.Thanks to her investments, Hans had accounts of several hundred thousand dollars in the defunct Panama account and about the same in the Switzerland Bank. He heard the busses leave for the football game and took a deep breath. Several screens and passwords later he accessed the Switzerland account.

"This can't be! Fuck! What is going on?". Hans was startled to see a zero balance on the account and a note it was confiscated by Interpol.Frightened, alarmed, he knew he could get to France on his credit card, call Chancellor Becker and reunite with Tilly.

"Just what I need!", he thought as Lady Vikki came into the office.

"You're not at the game?," he asked her.

"No. Where are you going, you look like you packed a lot of things. Not leaving here without me, are you?"

Hans nervousness answered the question for her. She decided now might be the time to take him out. His body will be burned beyond recognition in the explosion when she levels the building later anyway, she considered.

As she was deciding if she should reach in her handbag, pull out the gun and shoot him, there was a knock on the door. "Delivery. I need to talk to the Administrator."

Mikali entered, no uniform of course. He hit Lady Vikki who collapsed onto the floor, and he put a gun to Hans' head. " Which one of you is the Administrator? Get Angelo Olivanti in here now!"

Hans was shaking. "Who? I never heard that name."

"Bob. Robert O'Donnell."

"You want Bingo Bob?" Hans was taken aback, confused.

Mikali loomed over Lady Vikki and demanded to know what she knew about Bingo Bob. Confused and alarmed, Vikki was aware of Franz Worthermann's plan with Nazis, but didn't understand why some Colombian hitman was after Bingo Bob.

Cowering before Mikali, she blurted out, "Selingo Catering. They will have security pass for you to go to the game. Bingo Bob will be on the suite level. Please don't hurt me! I don't care what happens to him!" Hans looked at her in wonderment.

Mikali put the gun in her mouth. "One word. Just one word to anybody, and I will come back here and skin you both alive."

"What the hell is going on, Vikki? Who was that man? Why is he after Bingo Bob? What do you know about the catering? Who emptied my bank accounts? Where is the money?"

Lady Vikki just looked at Hans in disgust and again considered shooting him on the spot.

CHAPTER 54

WILLOWIST, SUPER BOWL SATURDAY 11 P.M.

"Something is wrong," George related to Sophia and Cat as they prepared for the extraction. "There is no activity at all in the German building."

Sophia looked over George's monitor. "It looks normal. All quiet. The Germans must be in bed for the night" as she observed empty cubicles. "And the camera in Hitler's room looks dark, no movement."

"Look more carefully, Sophia. If you watch it for a few minutes you will see its the same tape over and over. It looks to be live but its not. The Germans must have discovered my hacking and countered it with their own."

"I see what you mean."

"We have to abort the mission," George warned. "We have no idea what is going on in there, and you and Cat will be cut off from my help if the Germans are waiting for you."

Sophia and Cat shook their heads no at the same time.

"We're going in, George," Sophia said.

"We've spent months planning this operation, and Sophia and I know how to handle ourselves in a confrontation," Cat answered.

All three of them looked at the map of the interior for what seemed like the hundreth time. Sophia and Cat will access the abandoned bomb shelter from the woods trap door which was overgrown with bushes, shrubs and high grass, obvious that it hasn't been used in years. Or decades.

Once inside Sophia and Cat will make their way through the shelter to a steel basement door that gives access to the medical research building. The room they will enter is a boiler room only accessed by the Germans if there was a mechanical problem. Sophia was confident the boiler room noise will neutralize any noise from the plastic explosive she will use to open the door. She planned on just enough explosive to give Cat and her enough space to enter. The living quarters of the Germans were on the far side of the building, safely away from the boiler room noise.

"They will be sleeping, George. Cat and I have each been in far more dangerous situations.. Once inside we saw on your earlier video feeds where the power switch in the building is located. We'll turn the power off, and with our night vision glasses, AR rifles we will be fine."

"Plus we have the element of surprise," Cat added.

"I will keep trying to reestablish my connection and live feed to the building. What worries me is if the Germans discovered my surveillance and blocked it, they have to be suspicious that something is up," George said.

Sophia and Cat readied their weapons for their 3 am invasion and extraction of Adolf Hitler. The ATV they would use to go through the woods and field to get Hitler to airfield where a waiting plane would take him to Germany as per directions of Chancellor Becker.

"George, just text me if you go live again and alert me to any problems," Sophia suggested.

They discussed the plan after the extraction. Once Hitler was at the airfield in the custody of American and German agents,Sophia and Cat would join the Swoops bus to the game.

"DEA and CIA agents will move in and arrest the Nazi's still in the medical research building once we are out of there. Its important our undercover identities are not blown so that our government is not implicated in this mission in the event news of it leaks out.

If Worthermann shows up here, he will be arrested immediately, and the signal will go out to all law enforcement to arrest the Nazi cells. It will be a coordinated event in three countries. Germany, the United States and France. This will be a death blow to the neo-Nazi movement. All their leaders will be in prison, the cells wiped out," Sophia reminded George and Cat.

CHAPTER 55

SELINGO CATERING, SUPER BOWL MORNING

"Put your security passes in this bowl. Now! All cell phones too, " Angel bellowed. He searched each Selingo employee and handed out the passes to his men and women.

"Here's whats going to happen. You will be locked in that room. My men will be sitting out here and anyone messes with that door you will all be shot. Play along, and no one will be hurt."

Gus Dovanis tried to grab a gun but recoiled when Angel smashed his head into the cement floor, killing him. "Anyone else want to die?," Angel challenged. The Selingo employees retreated into the room, and Angel locked the door. He assigned two men with weapons to guard the warehouse, and as Angel left for the stadium he gave orders to shoot to kill if anyone tried to leave.

The Germans loaded their weapons next to the food, and the trucks left for the stadium.

A few minutes later the two German guards raised their weapons when Mikali and several other of El Gringo's Colombian men entered through the side door.

There was a tense standoff with each pointing a gun at the other.

The German who spoke English said "you have no business here. Get out!"

"Just give us O'Donnell, and we'll leave," Mikali answered. "Is he in that room, bitches?"

"Don't know who you are talking about. We have nothing to do with any O'Donnell."

" We were told O'Donnell was here." Mikali gave a signal to his men lower their weapons. The Germans did the same.

After a brief discussion the Germans and Mikali realized they had no conflict with one another. The German called Angel. "There are some Colombian guys here looking for one of the Willowist residents. It's nothing to do with our mission.

"Put him on, " Angel ordered. "Who are you?"

"We're here looking for Angelo Olivanti who is known now as Bob O'Donnell. El Gringo wants him."

Angel knew of El Gringo and quickly decided he did now want to start a war with a major druglord. Especially in the middle of the greatest event the Nazis are going to have.

"My men will give you security passes. Just stay away from any Germans in the stadium. We don't know who this O'Donnell is, and we don't care."

Mikali grunted "ok." His orders were to get O'Donnell. Not get into a firefight with German Nazis.

CHAPTER 56

WILLOWIST, EARLY MORNING HOURS SUPER BOWL SUNDAY

"Any news, George?" Sophia texted George from the wooded area behind the medical research building. "We're ready to go in."

"Be careful, Sophia. My hack into their system is definitely blocked. I have no idea what you will be walking into."

Earlier that evening Sophia and Cat readied for their descent into the abandoned bomb shelter. Dark clothes. Baseball cap with LED light. Pistols. A needle with the sedative to inject Hitler. A plastic explosive for the facility basement door.

"Just push through the bushes. The entrance trap door should open easily from our visit here last night to loosen it up," Sophia noted.

Cat used the metal tool and leveraged up the trap door while Sophia secured the rope they would use to descend into the darkened bomb shelter. The steps to the bomb shelter were decayed and unusable.

"For sure, no one was here in a long time", Cat observed.

Cat shimmied down the rope first, in between rock formations and landed at the door leading into the bomb shelter. At first it didn't open but Cat kicked it several times and entered with Sophia was right behind her.

"It's just like the map George showed us!," Cat exclaimed.

The first room was about the size of a family room in a suburban home. There were remnants of what was once furniture. Cat recoiled when dozens of a roach-like bugs climbed over her boots. "Yuk. I would rather face armed Germans than these monsters."

Moving carefully in the hallway they saw several bedrooms and what once was to be a kitchen area, now rotted away. A sound came out of a bedroom, and both drew their weapons. Sophia pushed open the door. "Its just a rock we must have shaken loose somehow."

"This place is creepy, Sophia. I can't imagine anyone living down here for any extended time."

"Remember the discussion we had about the Cold War in the 50's and early 60's? People were terrified of nuclear war, and they built these things in their backyards."

"There! That's the door into the main building!"

"I don't think we need to use an explosive, Cat. It looks to have deteriorated enough over the decades that we can force it open."

They carefully entered the boiler room, which, as George predicted, filled the room with a loud whining, electrical sound. Quietly, they climbed the steps leading into the kitchen area but the door to the kitchen was locked.

"Don't force it, Cat. I'll play with the lock." Sophia was able to use a tool she had in her backpack and wiggled the lock open.

The kitchen was completely dark. Sophia scanned her light around the room. "Nothing but dirty dishes in the sink. You would think with all their Nazi training they would keep a cleaner house," Sophia whispered. "Listen!"

"I don't hear anything."

"Exactly. Not even the refrigerator."

"All dark. Power must be off."

Guns drawn they walked down the hallway past the empty cubicles and the bedrooms.

"Sophia, I don't think there is anyone here!"

They turned their lights into the bedrooms. "Just untidy beds, like they were awakened from sleep. We better get upstairs, Cat! Use the back stairway."

There was an empty guard chair by the stairway. As they were walking up the stairs, the metal tool fell from Cat's backpack and clanged on the steps. Cat and Sophia froze. No sounds. No one shouting or coming running. They hurried up the rest of the stairs and entered the second floor hallway. The chair by the elevator was empty! No guard. They rushed into the hospital bedroom. Hitler's bed was empty!

"What the hell," Cat said. "How can there be no one here?"

Sophia called George, "The place is deserted. Even Hitler gone."

"I don't know, Sophia. Once they hacked into my system I couldn't monitor what's going on."

Cat to Sophia: "What now?"

"Now we go to the Super Bowl. Whatever Worthermann is planning at halftime is on schedule. We have to stop it!"

CHAPTER 57

BERLIN, EARLIER IN THE WEEK

Chancellor Becker was livid. Neo-Nazi protestors were rioting and looting in a quiet city neighborhood. Setting fires, smashing car windows, the young Nazi's carried signs and screamed "Down with Becker!" This was one of several popup riots throughout Berlin.

"Worthermann is behind this. Call an emergency meeting of the cabinet and get as many uniformed police there immediately, " he shouted to his Chief of Staff Brogan Fields.

"Right away, Sir." But Fields quickly texted Franz Worthermann to warn him Becker was sending police to arrest the protestors and by the time the police arrived the rioters were gone.

"Cancel the Cabinet meeting and let me alone, Brogan. I have to make a call."

Brogan Fields quietly stayed outside the closed door to the Chancellor's office, eavesdropping on the Chancellor's conversation,

"Mr. President, it's me. I think you need to be on alert, Worthermann is increasing the violence of the Nazi movement. Scattered protests, all aimed at me." Fields could only hear the Chancellor's side of the phone call.

"Where? How many? Can they be trusted? Ok, I don't need the details as long as you are top of it. I hope the operatives at Willowist you are telling me about know what they are doing. Next riot and I giving shoot to kill orders. Stay in touch."

Fields walked away from the door and placed a call.

"Franz, there are some operatives imbedded in a retirement home called Willowist. Yes, our facility is right next door."

"Ok, Brogan. Keep me informed on what that idiot Chancellor is doing. I will speed up our plans at our German facility there."

CHAPTER 58

HAMBURG

Worthermann called his field team near Willowist. In German he said, " We're going to move our man out ahead of schedule and keep him safe in the Selingo warehouse. Make sure to get our people working in the Willowist facility safely out of there and sent back here. I don't want them there when the place blows up. Be alert. I just got word the US has operatives in Willowist, and I will send details as they become available.

Worthermann's team had a van take the German workers to the airfield and a separate van take Hitler to the Selingo warehouse accompanied by a German doctor and a German nurse who were armed and trained in the use of weapons.

The plan was for Angel to take Hitler to the stadium and secure him in an ambulance in the underground garage at the stadium. Worthermann would be taken from the airfield directly to the stadium with security passes provided by Selingo. Everything was coming together. Angel would have his men eliminate Lady Vikki, then blow up Willowist and all the people in it. The Nazi cells would create chaos in the streets, rioting and shootings. All this would be carried out just as the triumphant return of Hitler and Nazism with him, and Franz Worthermann, the new Furher, emerged to a worldwide audience!

CHAPTER 59

WILLOWIST

Lady Vikki rubbed the side of her face where Mikali hit her. Hans was sobbing and kept asking her what was going on, where was all his money, why is some druglord after Bingo Bob.

"Shut up, you moron! You were taking off without me!" She pulled. a gun out of her handbag and aimed it at him. Shut up or I will blow your fucking brains out. Let me think a minute."

Hans sat on the floor, shaking his head and moaning over and over. "I won't leave you, Tilly", he blurted out.

"Tilly? Tilly! That whore. You are running away with her? She's dead, moron."

"Dead?" Hans began openly weeping. "Can't be. I love her. She loves me."

Lady Vikki grabbed a pillow from the couch and the muffled gunshot went right through Hans' heart as she whispered 'Heil Hitler'.

She was excited about her return to Germany, the triumphant rebirth of Nazism and her appointment to Herr Worthermann's cabinet.

Vikki was sure Worthermann's men had placed the explosives around Willowist by now. The detonator would be right where promised. The old biddies and viagra popping men won't be missed.

She considered blowing Willowist up now, not waiting for Hans' signal.

CHAPTER 60

WILLOWIST, SUPER BOWL MORNING

The Eagles organization sent a luxury bus, complete with a hostess onboard, for the Swoop Sisters and their friends. "The party bus" as the Swoops called it. The bus was to leave for the stadium early, and at Willowist, early is never a problem. Most of the senior citizen residents were up at dawn, lunch at 11, dinner at 4 pm, bed by 8 pm.

The bus would carry the Swoops and their guests directly to a back entrance at the stadium. The Swoops held a lottery the night of their last party for tickets to the game as only Sophia, Cat, Bingo Bob and the Viola and her crew were guaranteed seats. Along with the Swoops of course. Because the Swoops were guests of Eagles management, there were no security issues, and Sophia and Cat had no problem carrying their concealed weapons.

The Eagles had handily beat long-time rival Dallas Cowboys to advance to the Super Bowl in the championship game two weeks ago, and the Swoops had arranged for a tape of that game to be shown on the bus. The Jets were in the Super Bowl courtesy of an last minute field goal win over rival Miami Dolphins. The

Jets-Eagles game was considered too close to call although the Eagles were slight favorites because the game was in their home stadium. "Home field advantage," Lizzie explained to the residents who didn't follow football as closely as the Swoops did.

Bingo Bob's effort to sit next to Sophia failed when Cat beat him to the seat. "I'll trade you for the seat, Cat." "No thanks, Bob. Sophia is my chaperone today," Cat smiled. Unknown to Bob, Sophia had made Cat promise to take the seat next to her. "It's not that I dislike him, Cat. We have to stay focused on our mission. Right now Worthermann is in full command, and we are forced to react to whatever he is going to do," Sophia had said. "Bob might get in the way."

"It's going to be a great day!," Lizzie announced over the loudspeaker. "You all know the words to Fly Eagles Fly which the fans sing after every touchdown. Be ready. Our team will be scoring a lot of touchdowns. The Jets won't know what hit them!"

Mary Margret thought this last statement was hilarious and started wheezing with the infectious Swoop Sisters laughter. Everyone on the bus, including the driver and the hostess, began laughing. The hostess offered Bloody Marys, well received by all the guests except Sophia and Cat.

The day before Sophia and Viola had lunch together, as they often did, in the cafeteria. Ever since Viola had rescued Sophia from the time Alma locked Sophia in the steam room, Sophia and Viola spent as much time together as possible. They were both excited and happy to have reconciled.

"We should go on a cruise together, Sophia. Remember when we sat on a rug and pretended it was a flying carpet that would take us anywhere in the world. You always wanted to see London and I wanted to see Dublin."

Sophia answered carefully because she knew after the football game, she, Cat and George would disappear from Willowist. She also kept to herself how she has traveled all over the world, sometimes in combat gear and sometimes in undercover roles. A Muslim woman, an aged hooker, a fast talking real estate agent. "It's something to think about Viola, it has been absolutely wonderful to see you, to reunite and reminisce about our youthful days on the Iowa farms. I am committed to a return to the State Department in a limited capacity so my schedule is unsettled for now. No matter what, I love our friendship!" Sophia hugged Viola so tightly Viola sensed she might not be seeing Sophia for some time, maybe not again. Viola speculated her childhood friend might be dealing with a serious illness and resolved to stay in touch with her.

CHAPTER 61

SELINGO CATERING, SUPER BOWL MORNING

The two Bri soldiers pulled into the empty parking lot at Selingo's. "It's too quiet here for a catering operation for the football game later today. Keep your eyes peeled. Stay alert," the driver told the other soldier. "Park over here to the side of the building."

Inside the building the German soldiers saw the SUV on the security monitor. "Heads up, now what?", one whispered. "Is that drug dealer back?", referring to Mikali who had left.

"I don't think so. This is a different vehicle. Look! Two soldiers! Fuck, they're Bri!"

The Germans drew their weapons and hid behind some boxes as the Bri soldiers entered through the side door, with their weapons drawn.

"Hello. Anyone here? We just want to talk," the Bri driver shouted. Before he could say anything else, the Germans put a bullet in his head and demanded the other Bri drop his weapon, which he did.

"Get on your knees and put your hands behind your back. Now!"

The Bri soldier complied but refused to answer any questions. He was bound and gagged while the German soldier called Angel.

"What the fuck? Did any of those caterer people sneak a call for help?," Angel demanded.

"No, Boss. They are secure, locked up. This guy is Bri military."

"Damn. Why are the Bri here? How did they hear about this? Try to make him talk but don't waste a lot of time. If he doesn't cooperate right away, just shoot him. And secure the building in case anyone else comes, I'm sending more security to back you up. That Selingo's is like a fucking parade of people. I don't like surprises. Anyone else comes, shoot to kill, don't even bother to ask questions. Got it? Shot to kill. As soon as our operation is over, we'll get you out of there. Stay alert!"

The Germans ripped off the gag on the Bri soldier and began interrogating him by smashing his stomach and back with the butt of the rifle. "Why are you here, shithead," the German asked as he continued to punch and slap the Bri soldier. Finally, getting nowhere with the Bri, the German soldier shot him.

Inside the locked office room the Selingo employees huddled in fear. "Keep quiet in there or you'll be next," the German soldier warned the hostages.

CHAPTER 62

ON THE BUS

"Roll out the barrel, we'll have a barrel of fun. Roll out the barrel, we've got the blues on the run." Lizzie was standing next to the bus driver leading the Willowist seniors in song. The Swoops were in charge of the shopping and other bus trips and always kept it lively on board. Lizzie was especially animated on her way to what she referred to as "the most exciting day of my life watching the Eagles play the Super Bowl in their own stadium."

"Any news?" Sophia texted George. She and Cat knew they had to be alert, not knowing Worthermann's plans.

"I'm in their system, got it unblocked. Cannot fly a drone near the stadium, local security will shoot it down. Lots of chatter with the Nazi cells we identified, our police agents are all in place. They will raid the cells and arrest the Nazi's when we give the signal."

"Good. Make sure they understand to not move in until I send a signal to their central monitoring. Timing is everything. If our people move too soon it will scare Worthermann off. If he gets back to Germany our chance to arrest him is lost."

"The backup you requested are in place in the stadium", George texted. "All are undercover."

"Remind them under no circumstances do they do anything until I signal them. A shootout at the crowded game would end up with a lot of innocent people being killed."

Sophia and Cat's superiors,had made arrangements with stadium security for Sophia and Cat, who were armed, to enter a side door with no patdowns for weapons. The Swoops were to excited about the game than to worry about when Sophia and Cat would meet them at the suite.

"I'll go with you and Cat," Bingo Bob offered.

Sophia was firm, "No, Bob, we'll see you at the suite."

CHAPTER 63

THE STADIUM

Worthermann's Suite

The ambulance with Hitler was waved through security and parked by the rear loading dock door, where Worthermann and Angel were waiting, both dressed like security officers. The doctor and nurse and an armed guard would stay with the ambulance in a secluded section of the underground garage reserved for first responder vehicles. Worthermann and Angel would take the private elevator to their suite level.

"We have to make sure we thank our operatives here," Worthermann told Angel. "Everything went smoothly getting the Fuhrer here! It won't be long, Angel, and the revolution will begin." Angel grunted. "Boss, our guys at Selingos just texted that two Bri soldiers showed up but our guys killed them."

"The Bri? Warn our guys here to be alert. The American spies must be working with the Bri". Worthermann called Brogan Fields. "Angel heard the Bri are around here. What's going on?"

"The Chancellor has me locked out, he is talking to the American President. I haven't heard anything else. I think he is suspicious of me."

Worthermann hung up, agitated. "I don't care if we start a riot here. Shoot to kill if the Bri show up. No one is stopping us now," he barked at Angel.

Worthermann and Angel and two soldiers settled into the suite. Angel sent one of the soldiers to stand guard outside the suite door. "Too bad I don't like American football, the view here is great," Worthermann said to no one in particular. The players were stretching and exercising. Soon the doors would open and 80,000 fans would stream in. "The Americans need to get into soccer. When we take over the governments we'll ban nonsense like this. Angel, is everything in order?"

"Yes, Boss. All the stadium security in our suite level have been paid off and are out of here.Our soldiers dressed like stadium security are in place on the other side of the stadium and will take over the media room at halftime. They will announce all attention to be directed toward our suite. When you show Hitler and speak it will be carried live on the news worldwide. Our comrade cell members will erupt into the streets of the cities and the revolution will begin. As you make your announcement our soldier at Willowist will kill that bitch Vikki and the bomb will level the entire area. The plane will be at the airfield waiting for us."

"We'll take Hitler in the ambulance and leave here by the back access road. With all the chaos that will happen, we'll get Hitler back to Germany. Brogan will take dispose of the Chancellor. We will triumphantly return with me as the new Furher!"

Angel grunted his approval and spoke into his ear-piece, "Stay alert." The Germans in place in the stadium heard the message.

CHAPTER 64

THE STADIUM, WILLOWIST SUITE

The Swoops guided their guests to their suite. There were two bilevel suites one on each side of the scoreboard. Although there was a hallway, there were no other suites in this section of the stadium and access was limited to an elevator in the underground garage and several flights of stairs.

The food was plentiful, and the residents excitedly moved about the suite. No one paid attention that Sophia and Cat had not yet shown up. Except Bingo Bob. "Where's Sophia?", he asked Mary Margret. "She knows where to come, she and Cat were meeting some friends or something." "She'll be here, Bob. Relax and enjoy the moment!"

Bob played with the ring box in his pocket. He planned on giving her the ring at halftime, in front of the Willowist crowd. Bob was nervous. "Something is not right" he said to himself. "Sophia has been distracted. I have a bad feeling about today." He jumped when Lizzie unexpectedly screamed, "Go Eagles!" The stadium had filled and the National Anthem was playing. Air Force jets would do a traditional "fly overhead" in a minute as a show of patriotism, further exciting the crowd. Players would be coming out. Still no Sophia and Cat. Bob wondered "where are they?"

Sophia and Cat had security credentials and were walking with the crowd in the stadium. George alerted them Worthermann had placed soldiers undercover in the stadium, and Sophia and Cat were looking for signs of any Germans. "We can't let a shootout happen, Cat. Look at all these football fans. Families with kids."

Sophia's cell buzzed. "Sophia, I overheard the Germans on my computer wiretap, there is a lot going on." George continued, "Some druglord is looking for Bob O'Donnell. They are referring to him as 'Olivanti'. Two Bri soldiers were shot and killed at the caterer Selingo's. Best I can figure out is the Bri are looking for Worthermann."

"And El Grigno the druglord is looking for Bob," she replied, remembering the helicopter attack on the bike ride with Bob and his admission he is in the Witness Protection program, and we are all looking for Worthermann! Are you tapped into the Stadium security cameras?"

"Working on it, any minute now."

Sophia to Cat: "You go that way, the stadium is circular. I'll got this way. Text me if you see anything. We'll meet up right back here in a few. Keep your eyes open." Sophia and Cat wireless earpieces and could communicate with one another.

The sustained roar from the crowd alerted Sophia that the game was ready to begin.

CHAPTER 65

STADIUM, EL GRINGO

El Gringo, Malaki and two bodyguards flashed their security passes and entered through a side gate to the stadium. "Just look like you belong," the druglord said to his men, all dressed like civilians but carrying weapons. "Those Germans said the snitch will be on the scoreboard suite level. Just a bunch of old people. We'll grab Olivanti at halftime. A quick in and out and get him back to Colombia where he will find out what happens to snitches.Let's watch the game from here a few minutes. Anyone gives us a problem, shoot them.

"You seem to like football, Boss?", Malaki laughed.

"I hate Americans but I like American football. You've seen me watching games on our satellite televisions in the jungle camp."

CHAPTER 66

STADIUM, THE BRI

Commander Fetterman and his team considered the situation. They were at the entrance to the stadium, knew Worthermann and some aging Nazi were inside, but they had no tickets, no way to get in. They were armed but in civilian clothes.

"After we do our job here we'll go back to that caterer warehouse and finish those Germans who shot our guys," Fetterman sputtered angrily.

"What's the latest intelligence?" Fetterman asked his soldier. "Something's going to happen at halftime with Worthermann making an announcement. Same thing we heard before, nothing has changed."

"Have one of our guys create a diversion over there. The two of us can run through the ticket area and get lost in the crowd."

The Bri soldier approached the ticket area, screaming and waving his arms, showing a gun. The crowd ran wildly in all directions, security guards raced toward him and tackled him. Fetterman and his soldier jumped the gate and ran into the stadium, undetected by security.

CHAPTER 67

STADIUM, WILLOWIST SUITE FIRST QUARTER

The Eagles kicked off, and ball sailed through the end zone. No run back by the New York Jets igniting the crowd noise to as loud as that of a full blown stadium rock concert. As the Jets lined up, an Eagle player was off sides. The boos rocked the stadium. First and five yards for the Jets. The Jets quarterback was back to pass and sacked! More crowd screaming and cheering noise.

Sophia looked around the hallway on the suite level as she and Cat got off the elevator. Their suite was around a corner to the right. Worthermann's suite was around the corner to the left."That's strange. There is usually a security guard right at the elevator."

The crowd noise was so loud that no none in the suite could hear them knock, and Sophia texted Lizzie, "we're outside the door." No one paid attention to Sophia and Cat when they entered. Bob was on the lower level of the connecting suite and didn't see them. Viola and the Crew were sitting in the outside balcony of the suite where all the outside seats were taken.

"Everything looks ok here, Cat. Let's take a walk around the suite level and see if we can find Worthermann's suite. George said the stadium security cameras show Worthermann is on this level and has a guard outside the door. You and I need to take care of this on our own. If we wait and our backup people get involved there is more chance of a shootout. Right now you and I have the element of surprise on our side."

"Bingo! Sophia!" Bob shouted as he spotted her. "Sophia! Come sit with me."

Sophia waved him off before he could move towards her. "I'll be back. Cat and I are meeting friends."

Sophia and Cat quickly left the suite before Bob could make his way to them. Sophia's phone buzzed, and she took a call from George. "Cat! George just confirmed our target is in an ambulance in the underground garage. It's just him, a doctor, a nurse and one bodyguard. Let's do this! Stay alert!"

They raced down the hall to the elevator and went to the garage. When the guard heard the elevator ding he readied his weapon. "Anyone you don't recognize, shoot to kill" he remembered Worthermann's order. When the elevator door opened he saw Sophia and Cat with their guns drawn and got off a shot before Sophia killed him. Cat took a bullet and fell.

The doctor and nurse jumped out of the car, and the doctor shot toward Sophia. Her shot hit the doctor while nurse ran behind a parked police van. She shot toward Sophia who was now behind the ambulance. They traded gunshots until Sophia's shot hit the nurse, killing her. Sophia didn't see the doctor lying on the ground hurt behind her and aiming his gun at her. Just as the doctor was ready to shoot Sophia, he was felled by a bullet from Cat, who was still on the ground.

"I am ok, Sophia! My vest took the brunt of the shot."

Cat crawled over to the ambulance, pulled herself up and raised her gun toward the bedridden comatose Adolf Hitler. "This is for having my great grandfather crucified, you son of a bitch. Rot in hell!"

"No! Cat! Don't! It's not our call to take him out!," Sophia shouted.

"He murdered my great grandfather!"

"Cat. Let Chancellor Becker get rid of him. That's the plan. Don't do this. Please! He's evil. He's not worth you losing your career by violating our orders."

Unsteady, unsure Cat cocked the gun.

"Cat!"

Cat lowered the gun, crying.

"Lets get him in that storage room and put the bodies in there too. If the Germans see he is missing they may start shooting everyone in sight."

Cat recovered her composure and nodded. "Lets get Worthermann!"

The loud singing 'Fly Eagles Fly' meant the Eagles had scored a touchdown. All attention at the stadium was on the game.

Sophia and Cat looked at each other. The elevator was running.

CHAPTER 68

STADIUM, WORTHERMANN SUITE

"Angel, send one of the men down to check on our Fuhrer. There is interference with our radio contact with the doctor. He is not responding. It must be the stadium noise."

Worthermann decided it best to leave Hitler in the ambulance until a few minutes before the half. The halftime show involved dancers and a raucous rock group. Worthermann planned on his tech team to take over the media room and hack into the video and sound system during the show to broadcast his grand announcement.

"Angel? Did our man get down to the ambulance?"

"Same interference, Boss. I can't communicate with him. Should I go down?"

"No. I want you here. He'll report back soon."

Worthermann used his satellite phone to call Brogan Fields. "Are you with Becker?" "Yes. He is in his office watching the game. I'll take him out when you give the word."

"Don't do anything until after my announcement. I want him to see the new Third Reich with me as the new Furher before he dies. Then slice his throat."

CHAPTER 69

STADIUM, GARAGE LEVEL

Sophia raised her hand to Cat to stay silent and hide behind the ambulance. The elevator door opened and a German soldier stepped out. Sophia grabbed him from behind in a chokehold and twisted his neck.

"Take his phone, Cat. We will be able to monitor Worthermann!"

"Won't they come looking for him?"

"Maybe. Let's get his body with the others and get back to the suite."

CHAPTER 70

STADIUM

The Super Bowl was a wild offensive high scoring game. The fans were screaming and pounding their feet continuously, oblivious to the drama playing out in the underground garage. Eagles were behind 31 to 24 but driving toward another touchdown.

In Worthermann's suite, the mood was serious. "At the 2 minute mark, signal the doctor to bring him up, "Worthermann told Angel. "How can people watch this garbage," he added as he looked toward the field.

The party in the Swoop sisters' suite was in full swing with Viola and her Crew members were leading the cheers for the Eagles while on the lower level Bob yelled "Bingo" every time the Eagles made a good play as he kept looking around for Sophia. Lizzie was enjoying a cheesesteak, and Suzy was savoring a bowl of hot chili. Rosy had a pork sandwich, and the soft pretzels were a big hit.

El Gringo and Malachi were sneaking up the stairwell on their way to the Swoops' suite. "Good thing those Germans at the caterer warehouse gave us the security passes and intel where we will find Olivanti," El Gringo said. "The old people will be using the elevator, we'll stay on the stairs."

"What do we do when we get in there, Boss?"

"Just grab Olivanti and get out of here. Don't kill him but shoot anyone who gets in the way. I want him alive in Colombia. I am going to put him in a tub with ice water, cut off his toes, one by one and make sure he dies slowly."

Fetterman was on his way, now alone, on his way to the suite level armed with a pistol and information on the location of Worthermann's suite. He was determined to kill Worthermann no matter what happened to himself.

CHAPTER 71

Brogan Fields listened at the door of Chancellor Becker's conversation with the American President: "They will have him soon. The American operatives imbedded at Willowist have the target secure. Worthermann and all the Nazi cell members will be arrested simultaneously, thanks to our cooperation and Interpol. We have just prevented widespread bloodshed and riots. I found the leak in my Administration. Security will be arresting him any minute. I trusted him as my Chief of Staff."

Fields realized he had nowhere to go and quickly called Wortherman. "Get out! It's a trap! The Americans have the Furher! Get out of there Franz!" He could hear the security guards coming down the hall. "This is it. If I'm going down, so is Becker" he thought as he headed toward the Chancellor's office, gun drawn as he opened the door. No Chancellor! He quickly turned toward the back wall and as he aimed his gun at Becker, Becker fired first. Brogan Fields, trusted aide turned traitor, was dead.

CHAPTER 72

SUITE LEVEL: CHAOS

Eagles using a mix of pass and run excited the crowd to new heights of noise by tying the football game as the halftime was approaching.

In the Swoops suite there was cheering, smiling and high fives every time the Eagles made a first down or scored. Commander Fetterman pounded on the Swoops suite door, and Sophia, who had done several mission with Fetterman, opened the door.

"Sophia? What the hell? Where's Worthermann? What's going on here?" Sophia quickly explained the situation leaving out the fact that Adolph Hitler was in a secure room in the garage.

She gasped as she saw on the monitor Franz Worthermann, Angel and a German soldier coming down the hall, rifles in hand. Fetterman jerked away from her hand and entered the hallway where he was felled by a bullet from Worthermann.

"Cover me," Worthermann shouted at Angel as they ran toward the stairwell.

As they were descending the stairs being chased by Sophia and Cat, El Gringo and Malachi collided with them, knocking Cat down the stairs. El Gringo grabbed Sophia and held her at gunpoint as he dragged her into the Swoops' suite.

The Eagles had just kicked a field goal to take a 3 point lead close to halftime. On the other side of the stadium the American agents identified and cornered the Germans who were advancing toward the media room. At the "drop your weapons" command from the Americans, the Germans shot toward the agents but were felled by the barrage of return fire. The noise in the stadium drowned out the shootout.

El Gringo and Malachi burst into the suite, with Sophia being held at gunpoint by El Gringo.

"Give us Olivanti and no one gets hurt," El Gringo shouted about the noise. The stunned Willowist guests looked at one another in confusion. "Who is Olivanti?" Lizzie asked.

"Angelo Olivanti. Known to you as Bingo Bob O'Donnell. He's coming with me. He's a dead man! Now which one of you is Olivanti?"

Bingo Bob recognized El Gringo and started to make his way up the stairs from the lower level. But 77 year old Ron Asher stood up and said "I'm Bob Olivanti." Lew Bottelli stood up and said "I'm Olivanti." Dr. John Cooper said "I'm Bob Olivanti."

El Gringo shot Dr. Cooper and screamed, "Olivanti! I'll kill them all!"

Bob yelled out, "Don't hurt these people. I'll go with you."

Cat had crawled back into the suite from the hallway but before she could shoot Malachi, Suzy threw the bowl of hot chili in his face. While Malachi was painfully pushing the chili from his eyes, 80 year old Miriam Brandt kicked him in the groin, doubling him over. Lizzie smashed a silver punch bowl on his head knocking him out.

El Gringo started firing indiscriminately toward Bingo Bob, hitting him, Viola and Rosy DeStefano and several other Willowist residents. Cat recovered and returned to the suite but couldn't get a clear shot at El Gringo but was hit by a stray bullet. Sophia broke free from El Gringo's grasp, turned his gun on him and shot him.

"Call 911 and get some medics here," Sophia yelled to Mary Margret. "I have to get Worthermann."

Worthermann jumped into the waiting van but a car stopped on the access road blocked the path. Angel, driving the van smashed the stopped car aside as the van raced off the access road. Sophia took the ambulance, lights and sirens blazing, and went after Worthermann. She had Worthermann's van in sight as it moved toward the entrance ramp to Interstate 95 South. The van wildly sideswiped a Ford Focus and rode the beam past slow moving traffic onto the interstate. Sophia followed, with cars moving out of the way of the ambulance.

CHAPTER 73

WILLOWIST

At Willowist the Super Bowl parties were in full force. Big screen tv's, food stations. The Swoops had excited the residents about the game. The Swoops had even set up an area for residents in wheelchairs.

Lady Vikki was concerned Franz Worthermann, Brogan Fields and her other Nazi contacts weren't answering her calls and text messages. "What's going on?" Should I detonate the bomb?" Is someone taking me to the airfield?"

Vikki could see it was getting close to halftime and still no order from the Germans to blow up the retirement home. The detonator was hidden in the woods a few hundred yards from the main building. Her last order was to await a signal from Worthermann or Angel before starting the explosion that would level Willowist and kill all the residents.

"I'm not waiting any longer! Unless you text me to stop, this place is going to explode in five minutes" was her last text to Worthermann. Lady Vikki left for the wooded area and found the detonator in its hiding place.

"I'll blow this place into a million pieces and then wait at the airfield to be taken to Germany" she decided.

Vikki pushed the button and smiled as she looked toward the building. "I hate those old people. The rise of the Third Reich is coming! Heil Hitler!"

Nothing. No explosion. Vikki walked a little closer and pushed the button again. Still nothing. "Damn. Now what? If I touch the wires they might go off with me there." She texted Worthmann again "activated explosives, nothing happened. Send help."

Lady Vikki sat on a rock awaiting instructions and heard rustling in the woods. "Thank God you are here! Lets blow this place and get me on that plane to Germany", she shouted, still holding the detonator. A team of six United States marines burst out of the woods, grabbed her and handcuffed her." "What the…?" she started to say but was handcuffed and a hood put over her head. No one said anything to her as she was ushered onto an ATV and taken over a bumpy dirt road to the nearby airfield. Vikki was put on a plane bound for Germany. Not the triumphant return as a Nazi but as a prisoner facing murder, terrorism and enough criminal charges for her to spend the rest of her life in prison. Unknown to her, the marines had disengaged the explosive device and waited for her to attempt to blow up the building with all the residents in it. A terrorist act by a German national in the States that the United States and Germany agreed would be tried in an international court in Germany.

CHAPTER 74

STADIUM

While Sophia was chasing Worthermann, police swarmed into Worthermann's suite and medics attended to the injured at the Swoops party. Cat, Viola Lepere and Dr. Cooper were seriously injured and were taken to a local hospital. There were several minor injuries. Rosy DeStefano's arm was grazed and Peter Altieri had a minor concussion when the fell down the suite stairs during the El Gringo attack.

The Swoops offered to have all the Willowist guests quietly returned to Willowist but as shaken as they were, they decided to watch the end of the game.

The stadium continued to rock with cheering, booing and stomping feet in the grandstand as the Eagles and Jets kept up a high scoring Super Bowl. The attacks and shootings were confined to the isolated suite section and underground garage and went unnoticed throughout the stadium.

American agents removed Adolf Hitler and the German soldiers bodies and put them on a private jet to an airfield in Germany as directed by Chancellor Becker.

CHAPTER 75

PARIS, BERLIN, NEW YORK CITY,
PHILADELPHIA, WASHINGTON, D.C

The neo-Nazis gathered at their meeting places ready to begin Operation Third Reich. Heavily armed with Uzis, grenades and pistols, they were ready to take to the streets randomly shooting anyone nearby. The goal: chaos in the streets as Worthermann showcases a living Adolph Hitler to a worldwide audience at the Super Bowl. Plans were in place to assassinate public officials and take over news organizations.

What the Nazis didn't consider was there was another Operation Third Reich consisting of military, Interpol and police units that coordinated a surprise attack on each Nazi cell. The timing was synchronized with the arrest of Worthermann at the Super Bowl.

It was the handiwork of George Mattes' computer skills armed with information obtained from Tilly Miller and relayed to him from Chancellor Becker that led to the mass arrests and dismantling of Nazi cells. George had hacked into the private site created by Worthermann and uncovered names and addresses of the Nazis along with the physical location of each cell group.

The operation went smoothly and every Nazi was arrested except for the cell in Paris. The Nazis there were caught by surprise but were able to begin firing at the police units. A shootout started and several police officers were killed. One of the Nazis appeared at the door about to throw a grenade toward the police but a police sharpshooter hit the grenade, which exploded in the Nazi's hand. That explosion triggered other grenades in the Nazi's building, and it burst into flames, killing every Nazi inside. The Third Reich was not rising.

CHAPTER 76

ON THE HIGHWAY

Angel was weaving the van in and out of traffic at 80 to 90 mph, causing several cars to spin out and crash while Worthermann leaned out the window firing shots at Sophia and the ambulance. Traffic was at a complete standstill at the intersection of I-95 and I-476, and Worthermann's van nearly overturned as it bounced off the guardrail and then bypassed the traffic by going onto the beam sideswiping cars along the way and headed North on Interstate 476.

The chase continued at high speeds close to 100 mph, and Angel skidded the van onto the Schuylkill Expressway West and after a few miles exited to a huge mall parking lot. Sophia had been temporarily slowed by a car refusing to pull over for the ambulance and lost sight of the van. By this time George had a drone in the air and guided Sophia to a mall where a minute ahead of her Worthermann and Angle had entered Shoppers scattered when they saw the two Germans, guns drawn running down the mall. Angel turned and fired at Sophia, hitting her shoulder but she fired back, killing the drugloard's main enforcer.

Worthermann grabbed a teenage girl and put a gun to her head. "Put your gun down or this girl dies with me." Sophia began to drop her weapon but suddenly raised it and shot Worthermann, who tried but failed to fire his weapon at the girl as he collapsed, dead.

CHAPTER 77

HOSPITAL, UNKNOWN LOCATION

Sophia read the article under the byline Chrissy Rice to Cat, who was in the hospital bed recovering from a concussion and gunshot wounds to her arm and shoulder as well as assorted bruises from her fall down the stadium stairs:

"Would be dictator and former head of the German High Command Franz Worthermann was shot to death in a mall in the United States several days ago. While details are sketchy it appears Worthermann was the driving force behind an international Nazi movement attempting to bring a worldwide return to a new Third Reich with Worthermann as the leader.

German, American and Interpol agents raided various Nazi cells and arrested several hundred neo-Nazis under anti Terrorism laws. German Chancellor Becker lauded the governments of the United States and France for their cooperation to dismantle the terrorist organization. His popularity took a sharp rise as he released photos and documents of German nationals who were tortured and murdered by the Worthermann supporters.

The conspiracy by Worthermann and his military supporters to create chaos by assassinating local mayors and other political leaders was uncovered in time to prevent its success.

Most of the details of the events surrounding Worthermann's death are classified but it is known his plan was to murder senior citizens at a retirement home called Willowist in the United States. Worthermann's deranged plan to install himself as the leader of a reborn Third Reich endangered the lives of thousands of fans at the American Super Bowl football game.

Chancellor Becker thanked all the law enforcement officers involved and announced the arrest of numerous would-be Nazi leaders, including socialite Nazi sympathizer and 'traitor' to Germany Vikki Constantine, who was engaged in 'terrorist' acts. Becker called for 'peace and cooperation' among the world nations now that the threat of a return to the atrocities of Nazism was ended.

Although apparently unconnected to Worthermann and the Nazis, a major Colombian drug lord called El Gringo was murdered, apparently the victim of a rival cartel, according to information from a spokesperson for the Drug Enforcement Agency of the United States. Information found in his possession has led to the arrest of several corrupt customs officials and DEA agents, including Billy Green, one of El Gringo's top double agents.

"Good for her, Sophia! She had the exclusive story, and her career is taking off I am sure! I am sorry for the loss of your friend, Viola."

"Thank you, Cat, she was my childhood friend, I lost her friendship for years when she was angry at me, we reconciled when she saved my life the time I was locked in the steam room. I just wish she had gained consciousness long enough to know I was holding her hand, and she didn't die alone. You were also unconscious when they took you to the emergency room, I was just as worried about you! I am fortunate I just had some gunshot wounds that are healing nicely."

What's next Sophia?"

"It has been wonderful working with you, Cat. I will be leaving in a few hours for some well-deserved time off and wish we could stay in touch, but we both know protocol demands otherwise. George is already gone on his next assignment, I didn't even get to say goodbye."

"What about Bingo Bob?"

"By now he must know that you, George and I were working undercover. I do have feelings for him but I can't be involved in a romantic relationship. You know our lives are in constant danger and it wouldn't be fair to him to put him in that position."

Sophia and Cat discussed the after effects of the stadium shootout, and the story told to the Willowist residents how George, Sophia and Cat were military and were at Willowist to prevent a terrorist attack. "No one learned the truth about the Nazi movement, Hitler's presence and our role, thankfully," Sophia noted.

Sophia and Cat both in tears gave each other a final hug.

CHAPTER 78

WILLOWIST DAYS LATER

The stadium crowd never stopped the cheering and booing until the final second and were as exhausted as the players when the thrilling game was over. The 97 yard game-winning touchdown run by the Eagles running back in the second overtime has already gone down as the greatest run in Super Bowl History.

The Victory Party thrown by the Swoops was their best party ever. Viagra pills, Philly food, margaritas and visits by several Eagles players had the nurses on edge for fear the excitement would take its toll on the elderly residents. The remaining members of the Crew had a moment of silence and a final prayer for Viola and Dr. Cooper led by Rosy DeStefano, "May they rest in peace."

Willowist residents were never told how close they were to being victims of a bombing nor were they told why the former German research building was closed and the 99 year lease terminated.

The Gossip Room discussions had many questions and few answers. Where is Administrator Hans? Lady Vikki? Sophia? George? Cat? Of course the official story the residents were told is that Sophia, George and Cat prevented a major terrorist attack led by Germans in the medical research facility and that they were on assignment and would not be returning to Willowist.

"I always liked those three," Rosy DeStefano confided to the remaining members of the Crew, as she sipped on a glass of Merlot.

"Shut up, Rosy!" the other two crew members said in unison.

EPILOGUE

SOMEWHERE IN THE SOUTH OF FLORDIA

Sophia took a sip of her lemonade and continued reading her novel. She had always loved the romantic novels. Her Florida condo was smaller than her Willowist apartment but it looked out on the Gulf of Mexico and was in a private beach community. She had another month to decide whether to take another assignment or retire. Money was no problem for Sophia as she was paid well for the dangerous assignments she undertook and was not one to spend money on frivolous things.

"In a way I wish I could have had a relationship with Bob," she mused aloud, to no one in particular as she sat alone on the beach, enjoying the sunset. "Finally settle down and travel like a tourist, not a mission-oriented special operative. But would I miss the adrenaline rush of taking on the criminal element. Maybe."

Sophia was started out of her thoughts when she felt two hands from behind cover her eyes. She smiled when she heard that familiar voice: "Bingo!"

END

* 9 7 9 8 9 8 5 3 1 9 2 0 0 *